The Case of The Peculiar Portrait & Other Stories

T.G. Campbell

Cover central illustration by Peter Spells
Bow Street Society logo by Heather Curtis
Edited by Susan Soares
Copyright © 2018 Tahnee Anne Georgina Campbell
All Rights Reserved

Printed by KDP.

ALSO BY THE AUTHOR

TABLE OF CONTENTS

The Case of the Desperate Deed

I

Sulphurous smoke rolled along the platform as the shrill shriek of the train's whistle filled the vast interior of Charing Cross station. Though not widely considered to be as ornate as its King's Cross counterpart, the west-end terminus of the south-eastern railway was nonetheless impressive. Its vaulted, glass roof allowed sunlight to pour in, while its stone walls and tall windows gave it an almost cathedral-like appearance. As the incoming train slowed, its carriage doors' windows slid open and occupants' hands reached out and downward to lift the external handles. The doors were thrown open, despite the train being in motion, and youthful men in great, black coats, leather gloves, and bowler hats leapt onto the platform. Without pause, they continued their journey on foot as porters with sack trucks hurried past them to wait at the first-class, second-class, and luggage car carriages.

The high-pitched sound of grinding metallic brakes soon became lost in the raucous deluge of passengers. Men who carried caged parrots, and women in tattered shawls who carried babies and tugged underweight children along, emerged from the third-class carriages. Young ladies, attired in the black skirts, white aprons, and mop-caps of a maid's uniform under brown, woollen coats, also alighted, and weaved their way through the crowd to the first-class berths.

From second class came ladies in billowing, white blouses, long, brown skirts, and high-heeled boots. Sitting squarely upon their heads were black or yellow straw hats adorned with broad, black or brown ribbons, small feathers, and netting. Most were arm in arm with handsome men wearing suits of dark greens, blues, or browns, with waistcoats to match, under knee-length, black coats. Brushed black or blue bowlers, and trilbies, were their favoured pieces of headwear.

Lofty, black top hat-wearing gentlemen—middle aged or older—meanwhile sauntered from the first-class berths. Attired in perfectly fitted, high-waist trousers, plain, black waistcoats, and frockcoats, these gentlemen were typical of their class. Gold or silver tie pins and cufflinks caught the light as the gentlemen pressed the tips of their ebony walking canes against the platform floor and delivered brief orders to the porters.

The gigantic displays of dyed ostrich feathers, lace, flowers, and berries pinned to the immense hats of the first-class ladies were the first things to emerge from the berths when they alighted. Forced to duck as they did so, these same ladies had to either grip the frame of the door or accept the hands of their husbands to maintain their balance. The ladies' unnaturally slender waists, cinched by tight corset undergarments, were wrapped in fur stoles against the cold. Their heeled shoes, meanwhile, could only be glimpsed beneath their long, dark-coloured, bustle dresses. As their maids arrived, the ladies refrained from granting them any form of acknowledgement. Instead choosing to take the arms of their husbands, and walk alongside them to their private, horse-drawn carriages. The maids walked behind their mistresses, while an army of porters followed with the luggage.

One of the last first-class passengers to alight was an unaccompanied woman of forty years. Like her peers, she wore oversized headwear, complete with extravagant embellishments. The sleeves of her green, cropped jacket adhered to the fashionable style, whilst the hem of her high-waist bustle skirts stroked her buttoned, high-heeled, black ankle boots. Her complexion, unblemished by tan or hardship, was rendered paler by her dull, auburn hair, pinned into curls. An edition of the *Gaslight Gazette* newspaper was clutched against her breast as she descended from the train.

Taking a moment to steal herself, the woman went in search of the exit. A wave of travellers, keen to board the train she'd left, poured past on all sides. Ochre eyes, tinged by faint crows' feet in their corners, leapt from face to face as they darted past. Within moments, their features, clothes, and voices became a blur as the woman's mind struggled to register what she saw. Her fingers tightened upon the newspaper as, with shallow breaths, she picked up her skirts and hurried through the crowd.

The street outside provided no relief from the chaos, however. A melee of clattering horses' hooves, angry yells, trundling wheels, and jumbled conversations filled the air. The foul stench of manure and heavy dust from the innumerable coal fires of London also filled her nostrils and coated the back of her throat.

A long line of vehicles occupied the road in front of both Charing Cross station, and the adjacent hotel that shared its name. Private, enclosed, four-wheeled carriages collecting and despatching their passengers jostled for space against two-wheeler hansom cabs.

Unlike their private counterparts, the cabs were pulled by one horse. These lone animals were also brown in colour due to it being the most preferred among customers. Between its wheels, and resting upon the axle, was the main body of the cab with a wooden bench within a two-sided box. The ceiling of which also doubled as a canopy over the passengers' heads. Attached to the sides of the cab's main body were heavy, wooden doors with pointed middle sections to accommodate passengers' knees. These, coupled with the wooden canopy overhead, provided some shelter from the elements, and from any mud or spray the horse's hooves may kick up. The cab's drivers sat upon narrow seats, attached to the outside of the cab's back walls, which were elevated enough so they could see over both cab and horse.

For the more discerning traveller in London, whom hadn't the luxury of a private carriage, hansom and hackney cabs were the preferred choice, because of their relative privacy and social status. For those with even lighter pockets, however, such an option wasn't viable—especially when one had to make twice daily journeys between the suburbs and employment in the city. Walking, though healthier and cost-free, was also impractical in such instances. Thus many turned to the London Omnibus Company, and its many vehicles, for a financially sound travelling alternative. Most fares started at 1d (1 penny) or 2d (two pence) for part journeys, and didn't exceed 4d (a groat) or 6d (sixpence) for the entirety of a particular route. Even if one was returning home after dark, the omnibuses could still be relied upon. They ran from about eight o'clock in the morning until midnight.

The pavements on both sides of the street outside Charing Cross, where such omnibuses could be caught, were filled with would-be travellers vying to be the next to board. The medley of cargo did not help this limitation of space—from bulky laundry baskets to caged hens—these same travellers intended to take with them. At the crowd's front was a narrow, two-floored, open-topped vehicle painted red and pulled by a pair of brown horses. On its front were painted the words, "Royal Oak & Charing Cross," despite its destination being Bayswater. Other destinations, also painted upon its façade, included "Regent Street," "Oxford Street," and "Edgware Road."

The auburn-haired woman felt her stomach lurch at the thought of enduring the crowd and an omnibus journey. Turning toward a nearby hansom cab therefore, she smiled upon seeing it was vacant. No sooner had she approached, however, was she beaten to her prize by a hurrying young man. She lifted a hand and parted her lips, but the cab's doors closed and the driver whipped his horse into motion. The woman's hand dropped and, heaving a sigh, she moved along the queueing vehicles toward the hotel. None were another vacant hansom or hackney cab, however. Rubbing her temple as she returned to the omnibuses, she felt her heart pound once more.

Two yellow omnibuses had joined the red. Their façades painted with the words "Camden Town" and "Bull and Gate" Joining the crowd's rear, her eyes searched the faces of those nearby. Everyone was either turned away or—in her opinion—too frightful in their ugliness to address. Her cheeks and forehead became warm, despite the cold of the day, as her heart raced.

A third omnibus—this time green in colour—arrived. As it approached, its conductor—or cad as the job was more informally known—yelled out fares and reasons why his vehicle was the better choice. Once the omnibus had stopped, he jumped down from his narrow ledge at the vehicle's rear, and swung open a small, narrow door his body had blocked. Those at the crowd's head refused to budge as the omnibus's passengers descended the internal steps and exited. No sooner had the last vacated the vehicle though, was the cad taking monies from the new passengers.

Another glance toward the hansom cab rank revealed there were still none available. Heaving an even weightier sigh therefore, the woman approached the cad with trepidation. He was attired in a dark-brown, tweed suit with a brown, cotton waistcoat beneath. On his feet was a pair of scuffed, brown, leather boots. The knot of a black tie sat in the middle of a wide, starched collar, while the tie's tip was tucked under the waistcoat. A brown bowler topped his short, black, nearly combed hair as a black moustache graced his top lip. The top half of a small whip he held leant against his shoulder, while its lower half rested in the crook of his elbow. A smile lifted his weasel-like features as he laid eyes upon the unaccompanied woman. He said, "Good aft'noon, miss. A good choice yoo've made, comin' to my 'bus."

"Does it travel to Bow Street?"

"Dat it does, miss, dat it does." He raised the open palm of his other hand. "Sixpence, please."

The woman stole another glance behind her, but, alas, the crowd was too dense for her to see if any cabs had arrived. Relinquishing the sixpence to the cad therefore, she climbed inside and ascended to the exposed top deck. There were but four benches and all were occupied. Fortunately, a male passenger noticed her and slid across so she could take a seat. The cad, who'd pocketed threepence before putting the rest in his small, handheld box, slammed the door and climbed back onto his ledge. A quick pounding upon the door and the omnibus's driver whipped the dual horses into motion. The vehicle lurched forward and, as it was turned to join the vast throng of unfortunate cabs and carriages trying to pass Charing Cross, its top deck leant to the right. The woman at once gripped the bench and, tightening her incessant grasp upon the newspaper, didn't release it until she saw the sign for Bow Street.

As she ducked through the omnibus's back door, and held the cad's arm to alight, she expelled her held breath. Memories of carriages cutting across the omnibus's path, of malcontent passengers squeezing themselves around her, of the miasma of coal dust dirtying her face, and the malodourous stench of manure overwhelmed her mind. Yet, even as she stepped onto the pavement and took in her surroundings, she realised she'd still not reached her destination.

Standing at the corner of a multi-storied building made from gigantic, sandstone blocks, she referred to the *Gaslight Gazette* article. Some tall, yet narrow, wooden doors stood on the corner of the building. Above them was a pediment consisting of a flat shelf with stone scrolls supporting each end. Carved into a plaque between these scrolls were the words, "Bow Street Magistrates Court." As the woman concentrated on the article, trying to calm her racing heart as she did so, a dirty-faced woman in her early twenties emerged from the doors. She was followed by an equally dirty-faced young man. The former turned sharply to the right and strode down the street toward some steps leading to an arched doorway. Hanging to the right of this door was a white lamp marked POLICE. The dirty-faced woman said, "Dat was bloody daylight robbery!"

"You can't peach on a Beak to a Peeler," the

young man replied.

The young woman at once turned on him and asked, "Why not?"

"They're on the same side, ain't they? Besides, yoo got a fine, Sally. S'not like he clobbered yoo over the head and took your takings."

The auburn-haired woman, roused from her reading by the conversation, felt her stomach tighten all over again. Upon lifting her gaze, however, she saw the POLICE lamp and felt her tension ease. Resolving to seek assistance from an officer of the law, she tucked the newspaper under her arm and gave the dirty-faced couple a wide berth as she hurried past. Keeping her fast pace until she'd finally reached the base of the steps, her lungs felt like they were burning. Fortunately, the dirty-faced man had persuaded his companion to leave so the woman was at least given the opportunity to regain her breath. As she did so, however, she happened to glance down the street and saw the very place she sought. Her whole body felt like it had lifted into the air.

Walking to it, she found the exterior of the four-storied, semi-detached, red-brick building to be the epitome of domesticity. Its front door was oak, painted white, with floral carvings in a circular, raised-frame panel on its lower half, and a rounded stained-glass window of a yellow flower head in its top. The door stood back from the summit of steep, stone steps—commenced from the uneven pavement of Bow Street—thanks to the presence of a deep, white, wood-panelled porch. To the right of the door was a brass plaque. From the street, the woman could read the words engraved into the plaque. At once, she bounded up the steps and struck repeatedly upon the door.

"*Please…*" she said, utterly out of breath, as a young woman in her late twenties finally answered. "…*Please,* tell me this is the Bow Street Society?"

II

The parlour into which the auburn-haired woman was led was surprisingly sparse. A tête-à-tête sofa, with a high, triple balloon-shaped back, faced a large fireplace on the left side of the room. To the left of the sofa, facing the door, was an overstuffed armchair with a high back to match its counterpart. Both pieces were overstuffed and upholstered in a navy-blue fabric adorned with light blue, embroidered leaves. Both sofa and chair also boasted heavy, worsted fringes on their bases and bullions hanging from the fronts of their arms. Like the fringes, the bullions were made from brass-coloured cotton woven into a cone on the top, and given a fringe-like skirt on the bottom.

Aside from the seating, the only other items of furniture in the parlour were a low table and a bookcase in the corner. The latter's shelves were filled with leather-bound books—among them Charles Dickens, Conan Doyle, and the Holy Bible—and ornaments. One such ornament was a brass figurine of a young woman wearing a Grecian toga, and cradling a bouquet of wheat in her arms. A small scythe was in her hand. Beneath the table was a square rug that mirrored the seating's upholstery in its design. Its shortest ends also had brass-coloured fringes.

The walls of the parlour were covered in light blue, leaf design wallpaper with bronze gilt. Heavier than the cheaper alternative, the paper's additional benefit of the bronze meant the walls effortlessly caught the light coming through the sash window. Lumps of coal, orange with the heat, were in the iron hearth, to keep the room warm.

"I'm Miss Rebecca Trent, clerk of the Bow Street Society," the young woman who'd answered the door said as she turned toward her guest. Gesturing to the sofa, she added, "Please, sit down, Miss…?"

"*Mrs*," the auburn-haired woman replied as she lowered herself onto the spring-filled seat of the sofa and put her *Gaslight Gazette* on the table. Accepting the glass of brandy from Miss Trent, she took a sip before continuing, "Mrs Emillia Kinsley."

"In addition to maintaining the Society's records, I'm also responsible for hearing the problems of those wanting the Society's help. I decide, based on what I've heard, if the problem is one the Society would, or should, investigate on the client's behalf," Miss Trent explained.

Though of fair complexion, Miss Trent had blusher on her cheeks. That and red lipstick was the only makeup she wore. The longer portion of her chestnut-brown hair hung between her shoulders, whilst the rest was pristinely pinned atop her head with only a few, dangling strands to frame her face. The bustle skirts she wore were dark-brown in colour, with a few ruffles, and matched her long-sleeved, dark-and-light brown checked top. Its cuffs and neckline—the latter covering her bust but keeping her chest bare—had dark-brown fur trim whilst its fit followed the contours of the tightly laced corset she wore underneath. Thus, her waist was severely cinched, and her stomach was perfectly flat.

"I'm not entirely certain it *is* a problem your group would look into, Miss Trent."

"If you could describe it though, Mrs Kinsley, I may assess its suitability. As you may already be aware, the Bow Street Society was created to ensure justice is served when the police either can't or won't investigate. Unlike the police, however, our civilian members are at liberty to investigate both private and criminal cases if I deem it's appropriate for us to do so. Provided your commission falls anywhere under this remit, Mrs Kinsley, I see no reason why we wouldn't accept it."

Mrs Kinsley kept her eyes fixed upon the brandy glass, her thumb rubbing its side. A rhythmic ticking could be heard coming from the grandfather clock in the hallway. Memories of the unfathomable melee of sounds on Bow Street, and the traumatic journey to the Society's headquarters, dissolved in her mind as the brandy calmed her nerves. Soon enough, she pulled forth her recollection of the series of events which had compelled her to go there in the first place.

"I am gladdened to hear you say such, Miss Trent." Mrs Kinsley sighed and took a second sip of brandy. "For the Metropolitan Police certainly can't help me; no crime has been committed yet."

"Yet?"

Mrs Kinsley nodded and left her chair to retreat to the window. Miss Trent intentionally kept her pencil poised, her tongue held, and her brown eyes watching her guest's back. "I do not *wish* for it to be so," Mrs Kinsley continued. "God knows how I've tried to dismiss my fears as idle foolishness. No matter how vehement my efforts though, my fears invariably overwhelm my senses the moment I see my brother's face." She turned away from the window and sat on the sofa. "I am a woman of wealth. My late husband's estate provides me with a generous annual allowance. An additional, smaller sum was issued by his insurance brokers upon his passing. I used it to invest in my brother's fledgling jewellers' shop in Cheapside."

"May I ask the name of his shop?" Miss Trent asked as she started her shorthand notes, thus drawing Mrs Kinsley's gaze to her pencil.

"*Kinsley's Jewellers*. My brother wanted to honour my late husband and me. Lorne—my brother, Mr Lorne Cheshire—has a natural talent for diamond cutting and setting. His pieces, which he designs himself, are beautiful. Regrettably, his talents don't extend to sound business acumen, and the shop has floundered."

"Does he have any other financial obligations? A wife, children, perhaps?"

"No. Our parents died some years ago, and Lorne has never married." Mrs Kinsley paused momentarily to allow Miss Trent time to write. "My brother isn't a man of vice, Miss Trent. Neither tobacco nor spirit passes his lips, and women are not a distraction. Instead, his sins are ambition and an inability to resist temptation. A flawless gem's allure is ample provocation for him to part with a small fortune. At first, his requests for financial aid came but once a year. Then, they were *weekly.* Soon after, he became so reliant upon my assistance, he took repeated, unnecessary financial risks. He was a *drain* on my income, Miss Trent. *Please*, do not think I'm unfeeling toward his plight, however. The fear I felt for him, and still feel to this day, is *crippling*. Yet, what use would I be to him if I, too, were thrown into destitution?"

She lifted a trembling hand to her brow.

"Eventually, I *had* no choice but to refuse his request. Rather than discourage his behaviour, though, as I'd hoped, it instead led him to moneylenders. Now, he owes indeterminable amounts in loans—loans he has no hope of repaying."

"This he has told you?"

"Yes. Already he has been threatened with violence against his person, and debtors' prison. If he's held in such a place, he'll lose his shop and all he has worked for." Putting her brandy on the table, Mrs Kinsley again rose to her feet, this time to pace back and forth in front of the hearth. "I could pay the debt, but what then? My brother has repeatedly broken his promises to me."

Approaching Miss Trent, she removed a glove and held out her hand. A substantial ruby, set in the centre of a diamond cluster, adorned a gold ring on her wedding finger. "This is one of only a handful of gifts my husband bestowed upon me in his lifetime. Lorne showed great interest in it during his last visit, when he'd only ever given it a passing glance prior."

"I see," Miss Trent replied, her tone made heavy by her suspicion of a likely, albeit assumed, motive behind Lorne's behaviour.

Mrs Kinsley's voice echoed this weight as, with tear-filled eyes, she urged, "*Please,* say you shall help me?"

"*We* shall." Miss Trent stood and grasped her

client's hand. "The Bow Street Society accepts your case, Mrs Kinsley. Mr Snyder, our driver, will take you home in our carriage while I arrange for one of our members to visit upon you later today."

Mrs Kinsley gave a loud sigh as the tension at once dissipated and her entire body relaxed, causing her to crumple like a marionette. Miss Trent dove to catch her mid-swoon, but Mrs Kinsley's weight was far greater than her own. Fortunately, Miss Trent was somehow able to regain her footing, and maintain her grip long enough to lower her client back onto the sofa.

III

Slender fingers lowered a cigarette, as green hues regarded Miss Trent through dissipating smoke. Despite the gas lamps' light being weak, Miss Trent could nonetheless distinguish his high cheek bones, smooth jaw, and golden-blond curls. Attired in a black suit with white cummerbund, bowtie, and frilled shirt, the smoker lounged upon a *chaise* semi-hidden by a five-panelled changing screen. Miss Trent stood, with hand on hip, at the screen's edge.

To her right was an oak, desk-like table with three deep drawers at either end. Its surface was highly polished, whilst its edges and drawer fronts depicted hand-carved stars, moons, and other signs from the zodiac. Tubes of grease paint, boxes of talc, and bottles of black hair dye lined its back edge. A cream ceramic bowl, with hand-painted, Chinese-style decoration, and a matching jug stood in it, were placed in the desk's centre. Lined up to the bowl's left were combs, hair scissors, nail scissors, and nail files. A bar of lavender-scented carbolic soap, a box of powdered talc, chalk dentifrice in a round, ceramic box, and a wooden toothbrush, with horse hair bristles, were lined up to the bowl's right.

Mounted upon the plain, dark-blue, papered wall directly above the desk was an immense mirror in a gold, gilt frame. This had the forms of two women, barely covered by togas, holding up vases of grapes on its left and right edges. On its top and bottom edges were simple scrolls and leaf embellishments.

The only door was closed, but the muffled sounds of laughter and music nonetheless reached their ears. Loud applause shortly followed thereafter. Miss Trent noted it wasn't nearly as raucous as when her companion had spat the bullet into his hand to prove he'd 'caught' it with his teeth. Unlike everyone else in the Paddington Palladium's auditorium, she hadn't believed it. Instead, she'd applauded his showmanship and skilled manipulation of his audience's emotions—a manipulation they'd been all too eager to submit to.

"It is not a question of whether it is preventable," the smoker said. "But rather if I *want* to prevent it."

"You agree with my suspicion Mr Cheshire may attempt to steal the ring, then?"

"But of course. Desperate times call for desperate deeds."

"Exactly, this is why I've assigned you to Mrs Kinsley's case. Danger is an old friend of yours, and this could prove dangerous if his situation is as dire as she claims." Miss Trent smiled. "I understand your reluctance, Mr Locke. Being a man of questionable habits yourself, you undoubtedly feel a kinship with Mr Cheshire. Unlike you though, he has yet to use his thieving skills for the greater good. Besides, you're the only Society member with those skills, and your assignment to this case *isn't* a matter for debate."

"I never thought it was." He smirked, reuniting the cigarette with his lips. "I must admit though, I *am* intrigued by the whole affair." He, again, regarded her through a cloud. "When is the alleged theft expected to take place?"

"Mrs Kinsley didn't know, but she's invited her brother to dine at her home this evening, along with some mutual friends."

"Then I, too, must attend." Standing, he crossed the room and crushed his cigarette in an ashtray upon the desk. Next, he combed his curls and straightened his bowtie while looking in the mirror.

"I will telephone you with her address," Miss Trent said as she watched his preening. "Please remember she is our *client,* Mr Locke. I don't want any complaints of improper suggestions."

"Come, come, Miss Trent. You know me better than that. I am a perfect gentleman. Besides…" His eyes almost twinkled as he smiled at her reflection. "I have *never* had any complaints before."

IV

Iridescent and flawless were but two of the adjectives
which came to Mr Locke's mind as he inspected the ruby
and diamonds through a loupe lens. The lens was mounted
into a round, brass frame held aloft from the table by three
thin legs. A mantel clock ticked, and dark-grey skirts
rustled, as Mrs Kinsley's elderly housekeeper moved
about the morning room lighting the gas lamps. No sound
was emitted by Mr Locke, however, despite his turning
the ring within his fingers. Emillia Kinsley, who sat by the
hearth, watched him with keen interest.

    The morning room was situated on the ground
floor of the townhouse she'd shared with her husband. Its
décor was modest, yet tasteful. Nile-green stripes
interchanged with olive-green ones on the wallpaper while
plain olive-green wallpaper adorned the ceiling. The
window, which overlooked the darkening street, was bay
in style. Heavy, Nile-green curtains were pulled across the
three panes of glass to keep out the cold. The table at
which Mr Locke sat, stood in front of the window. Made
of rosewood, it was covered by a dark-green, cotton cloth
to guard its surface against any scuffs or scratches. A
bouquet of wax flowers, housed within a thick, glass
dome, stood in the table's centre. At its far edge was a
kerosene lamp with a bulbous, brass base and round,
frosted-glass shade. The shade had an open, glass chimney
as part of its construction to allow the heat from the
interior flame to escape—thus preventing the possibility
of the shade cracking or exploding.

    Four chairs, including the one Mr Locke sat upon,
surrounded the table. A plain carpet, of matching colour to
the cushions and tablecloth, completely covered the floor.
The sofa, upon which Mrs Kinsley sat, was wide enough
for two and had a solid, rosewood frame. Semi-stuffed
cushions, also Nile green in colour, covered a panel in the
sofa's back and seats. The arms had only stuffed rolls in

the middle of their tops. Overall, the piece of furniture could be highly recommended if one had an aching back.

"Your husband had an excellent eye for gems, Mrs Kinsley," Mr Locke remarked as he straightened in his chair to meet her gaze. "I trust you have a paste replica of this ring for protection against its theft whilst travelling?"

"I do. My brother could undoubtedly identify its flaws, however. Did Miss Trent not inform you of his profession?"

"She did, but I am not proposing you wear the replica this evening. No, I am proposing you place the replica into my possession, so I may use its superficial resemblance to my advantage, to thwart your brother."

"I don't see how you possessing the replica will prevent my brother from stealing the genuine ring from my finger, Mr Locke. Yet, I shall nonetheless do as you ask."

"All will become clear after tonight, Mrs Kinsley." Mr Locke dismantled the loupe lens and returned it to its box. "You have my word."

V

"May I introduce Mr Percival Locke," Mrs Kinsley announced to her friends gathered in her parlour upon Mr Locke's arrival. One such friend—a man no younger than sixty with bushy, grey whiskers and a moustache and beard to match—extended his hand.

He said, "I say, sir, you're not *the* Percival Locke, are you?"

"One and the same, sir," Mr Locke confirmed.

The elderly gentleman's wife—a lady in her late fifties wearing a modest, dark-brown, silk, bustle dress with white, frilled cuffs and collar—gasped. Smiling, she waited until Mrs Kinsley had introduced her and her husband before asking, "Will you show us a trick, Mr Locke?"

"By all means," Mr Locke replied, retrieving a deck of cards from his dinner jacket. Mrs Kinsley, who had noticed her housekeeper bringing another guest to the parlour, excused herself to greet them.

Like the morning room, the parlour had been decorated with great taste and sophistication. A stone fireplace, with a broad mantel shelf and pillars framing the hearth, dominated the right side of the room. Set in the centre of the mantel shelf was a clock boasting a large, ceramic face with Roman numerals painted in black around its edges. Housed within a brass casing, the clock stood on a broad pedestal of the same material, with brass flowers and leaves framing the face. Mounted upon the wall above the fireplace was an oil painting of a handsome gentleman in a British Army officer's uniform. Mr Locke could only assume the man in the painting was the late Mr Kinsley.

The walls of the parlour were decorated with burgundy wallpaper depicting an embossed, scroll design. The floor was meanwhile covered by a plain, yet plush, burgundy carpet. Due to night having drawn in, along with the cold, both a fire and the wall mounted gas lamps had been lit. A three-piece parlour suite, consisting of two overstuffed armchairs, a gentleman's chair, and a two-seater sofa formed a circle in front of the fire. An immense fireguard, constructed from a solid piece of oak elaborately carved with flowers and leaves, stood in front of the roaring fire. A set of brass pokers and a pair of brass tongs stood within a stand to the right of the fireplace. Two oak cabinets, with large glass panes in their doors' central panels, stood to the left and right of the fireplace. Within the cabinet on the left was a silver dinner service complete with plates, gravy boat, fish knife, and goblets. The cabinet on the right, meanwhile, displayed the finest cut glass. Wine glasses and decanters, blown with a diamond design in their sides, lined the shelves. Vases and serving platters also occupied the space.

Mr Cheshire was noticeable by his absence. According to what Mrs Kinsley had told Mr Locke, prior to her introducing him to her friends, the would-be thief was not only half an hour late, but had neglected to send a reason for his delay ahead of him. Aside from it being wholly impolite, Mr Locke considered it an unnecessary complication to his plan. He was therefore pleased to catch, out the corner of his eye, a lone gentleman entering and greeting Mrs Kinsley with an embrace.

To an outside observer, Mr Locke delighted his fellow dinner guests with a card trick. Anyone who knew him, however, would have noticed he had discreetly placed himself opposite the door with the shortest dinner guest—the elderly gentleman—facing him. Thus, he'd supplied himself with an unobstructed view of the new arrival. In Mr Locke's opinion, he could've been no older than his late thirties. Wavy, chestnut-brown hair, streaked with blond, was carefully parted down the centre. Unlike Mrs Kinsley's friend, his fair-skinned face was clean shaven, an increasingly fashionable sight at the time. While he shuffled the cards, and explained the aim of the trick he was about to perform, Mr Locke simultaneously watched the further interaction between Mrs Kinsley and her brother.

Lorne Cheshire held her hand—the one with the ring—between his own as, with profuse regret, he explained his delay. A customer, Mr Locke overheard Lorne say, had come to the shop in the last remaining moments of its usual opening hours to purchase a necklace. Mrs Kinsley smiled, and imparted her words of relieved congratulations, while resting her other hand on his.

When they broke contact a moment later, Mr Locke observed Mr Cheshire's fingers slide over his sister's knuckles, and plunge into his frockcoat's pocket. A glance to Mrs Kinsley's finger confirmed the ring's absence to Mr Locke, though the poor woman had yet to notice. Being only halfway through his trick, Mr Locke knew he couldn't excuse himself without causing confusion. As Mr Locke had expected though, Mr Cheshire ventured further into the parlour rather than cause a stir with a premature departure of his own.

"How *do* you do it, Mr Locke?" the elderly gentleman's wife asked once the trick had reached its pinnacle.

"With many hours of practise, and *excellent* sleight of hand, my dear lady," Mr Locke replied with a smile as he put the cards away.

The small group chuckled, and he excused himself from their company. As Mrs Kinsley's maid offered him refreshment from a tray of wine glasses she'd been carrying about the room, Mr Locke tracked his target. Seeing Mr Cheshire was momentarily alone, Mr Locke took a glass, thanked the servant, and crossed the room. Rather than slow his pace though, he feigned distraction, and walked straight into Mr Cheshire, tipping his glass as he did so.

"Do you *mind*?!" Mr Cheshire yelled, as he stepped back and stared down at the crimson stain. The other guests at once strangled their discussions and gawked at the scene.

Mr Locke meanwhile turned away, put down his empty glass, and retrieved his handkerchief. Without waiting for permission to do so, he gripped Mr Cheshire's jacket, held it open, and rubbed at the stain. "Oh, I do *beg* your pardon, Mr—?"

"Cheshire. Who the *devil* are you?"

"Locke, Percy Locke. I truly did not see you standing there. I was on my way to speak with Mrs Kinsley—"

"What's happened?" Mrs Kinsley herself enquired as she approached. "Lorne, are you all right?"

"Yes. Mr Locke spilt wine on my shirt." Mr Cheshire pulled his jacket from Mr Locke's grip. "My *best* shirt."

"Please, allow me to recompense you," Mr Locke said, putting away the soiled handkerchief, and taking some money from his other pocket.

"Your money shan't hide my stained shirt at dinner." Mr Cheshire growled. "I'll have no choice but to return home and change."

"In that case, allow me to transport you. My carriage is but a stone's throw away, and its thoroughbred horses shall have you home and back again in no time at all." Mr Locke took hold of Mr Cheshire's arm.

At once, the jeweller's tense jaw relaxed, his eyes widened, and the colour drained from his face. "No, thank you. It won't be necessary."

"I *insist,*" Mr Locke said, his hand already guiding the man toward the door. "It shall only take a few minutes."

"Please, go with him, Lorne," Mrs Kinsley urged, her expression holding more concern than the situation called for. Struck by this, Mr Cheshire hesitated, but couldn't see any malice in his sister's eyes. Her subsequent meek smile, and momentary grasping of his hands, further weakened his fear. It disappeared entirely when she said, "We shall await your return before serving dinner."

"Thank you, Emillia," Mr Cheshire replied, and he and Mr Locke departed.

Mr Locke maintained a short distance behind Lorne as they descended the steps to the pavement. He therefore had a perfect view of him closing his fingers around a small object within his pocket. Yet, Mr Locke chose to wait to act, for he knew such a confrontation made this close to the house would only serve to create a scandal too damaging for all concerned.

Mount Street, where Mrs Kinsley's residence was located, had been categorised by Booth's Poverty Map of 1889 as being "upper middle and upper classes wealthy." Due to this elevated status, those who lived on Mount Street held an unspoken expectation their neighbours should be as respectable as they. Any who conducted themselves and their business in such a way as to mirror the residents in Booth's "vicious, semi-criminal" areas, e.g. Whitechapel, could therefore expect to be shunned by their peers. A fate considered worse than death by members of the wealthier London populous.

The perfect opportunity came when they were halfway down the deserted street. Mr Locke's carriage was under one of many gas-fuelled street lamps which lined the cobbled road. The house it parked outside was in complete darkness, as was the residence on the opposite side of the street. Those adjacent to them had their curtains drawn. The only light being emitted from these buildings were kerosene lamps within attic rooms. The moon was covered by dense cloud, too. Therefore, Mr Locke thought it unlikely either he or Mr Cheshire could be seen by anyone looking out these windows at the street below. Lastly, Mr Cheshire's attention was on Mr Locke's carriage rather than on Mr Locke himself.

The jeweller was still agitated, however. Mr Locke suspected this agitation would only increase once he revealed his hand. The possibility of speaking to Lorne in the carriage was therefore dismissed as being too risky—at least for the time being. Instead, Mr Locke made a single, long stride and sidestepped while turning toward him—thereby blocking his path. Mr Cheshire at once jolted backward, stumbled a little, and parted his lips to demand an explanation. His words caught in his throat, however, when he saw the unmistakeable glint of diamonds in Mr Locke's raised hand.

Without any consideration of consequence, he retrieved a ring from his own pocket, and hurried to the light of the street lamp to inspect it. His jaw dropped, and his eyes widened, when he recognised the unmistakeable signs of the 'gems' having been moulded rather than cut. He searched his memory. The ring he'd taken from his sister's finger *had* held a *genuine* ruby and diamonds. He'd made certain of the fact by discreetly inspecting them whilst holding her hand! "How…?"

"I saw you slip it from your sister's finger and drop it into your pocket. I must say, you showed *excellent* sleight of hand. When I spilt my wine upon your shirt, I executed a far superior move by slipping my fingers into your pocket and retrieving the ring. The paste replica was dropped into the same pocket when I reached for your jacket. You would not have felt anything on either occasion"

"But… Why?"

"Your sister hired the Bow Street Society, of which I am a member, to prevent your theft of her ring. She has made us aware of your financial difficulties, associated with your jewellery shop in Cheapside, but also of your talent for creating beautiful pieces. Rather than summon the nearest police constable, and demand your immediate arrest for attempted theft, though, I instead wish to present a proposal for your consideration."

"Why should I trust you?" Mr Cheshire asked, his eyes narrowed, as he looked between Mr Locke and the ring. "I have *very* violent men demanding payment from me, Mr Locke. I can't afford to surrender the ring to you. My life depends upon my selling it."

"On the contrary, Mr Cheshire, your life depends upon you doing, precisely, what I say."

Mr Locke closed his hand around the ring, waited for a heartbeat, and unfurled his fingers to reveal air. Mr Cheshire's chest tightened and a high-pitched cry of despair burst from his lips. He lunged for Mr Locke, but was thwarted in his attack by a firm shove. His eyes bulged and he found himself reeling backward, unable to catch his breath. Wheezing while grasping his chest, the jeweller kept his distance

"Following a brief return to your residence for the purposes of changing your shirt—your transportation being my own carriage—you shall return to your sister's home and take full advantage of her generous hospitality. Tomorrow morning, you shall visit upon me at the Paddington Palladium, where I shall have a written agreement for you to sign. In exchange for an initial lump sum, which you shall name in accordance with the amount owed to the moneylenders, you will create pieces to be worn by the ladies on stage. I shall pay you a monthly retainer to create pieces, as and when I request them, as gifts for my wife.

"Additionally, you shall be granted the opportunity of an interview with Miss Trent, clerk of the Bow Street Society, for membership. I am quite certain she shall deem your expertise with jewellery invaluable, and likely to be of use in future cases. So, are we in agreement?" Mr Locke extended his hand.

The jeweller, whose rage had eased and dissipated the more he'd heard of the proposal, stared at him, agape. "I… I don't know what to say, Mr Locke…"

"Say you shall accept, and endorse our gentleman's agreement with a handshake."

"Yes… Yes, of *course* I accept. Without a shadow of a doubt, I accept!" Mr Cheshire exclaimed, grasping Mr Locke's hand in both of his own and shaking it vigorously. He wasn't as sensitive as his sister, though, so Locke wasn't obliged to rescue him from the consequences of a faint. Instead, he could admire his relieved smile, which mirrored his namesake's from Lewis Carroll's *Alice in Wonderland*.

"You can't begin to know what this means to me, Mr Locke. You have saved my business—my life! How can I ever repay you and the Bow Street Society?"

"Your cooperation with my terms, and your sister's gratitude, is payment enough for me. Miss Trent will naturally expect payment for the service provided by the Bow Street Society, but your sister is our client, not you. You, Mr Cheshire, will instead become one of *us*. Consider this the beginning of a long and successful business arrangement between you and the Paddington Palladium."

"I *will*, Mr Locke. Oh, I *will*!"

The Case of the Scandalous Somnambulist

I

Globules of rain followed their predecessors' tracks down the window's panes while their fellows battered its ledge. On the street outside, the incessant volley of horses' hooves and carriage wheels whipped up puddles—saturated with soot and liquefied manure—to hurl them upon the feet of inattentive pedestrians. Watching one such occurrence through the deluge of rain against glass was Mr Warwick Truman.

Despite the flawlessness of his fair complexion denoting his twenty-one years, his receding hairline added twenty-one. His remaining hair was burnt oak in colour, swept back over his crown, and combed down between his ears. Vivid, amber-coloured eyes took in the disgruntled pedestrian's reaction as, with a deep baritone, he began, "I'm not a jealous man." Resting his hand on the window ledge, he half-turned toward a woman in an overstuffed armchair by the fire.

Though seven years older than Mr Truman, her superficial age was at least ten years younger due to her fair skin and slim build. While his hair was receding, her chestnut-brown tresses were abundant in both length and volume. Their majority hung between her shoulders with the remainder pinned into a pile of tight curls atop her crown. Their choice of attire also provided credence to this contradiction; he had opted for the conservative, black frockcoat, unembellished, brown waistcoat, and oversized, black cravat of the older generation, while she wore a deep-red bustle dress with plunged neckline attached to a black, net panel to preserve her modesty. The sleeves of her dress ended at her elbows, but black, lace trim cascaded at least a foot from their cuffs. Further trimming—of the same colour and material—adorned the skirts' hems and front panel. Though unfashionably straight in their overall shape, her dress sleeves' shoulders clung to hers with only an inch to spare. Her dark-brown eyes were stoic as she returned Mr Truman's gaze.

Sliding his fingers from the ledge as he moved away from the window, he continued, "I dare say many see me as weak because of the freedoms I give my wife."

A tête-à-tête sofa, with a high, triple balloon-shaped back, faced the large fireplace. Retaking his seat upon it, he looked to his untouched cup of tea sitting upon the low table in front of it. Beneath the table was a square rug of navy blue with light-blue leaves. The seating mirrored its colours which, alongside the wallpaper, created a chill within Mr Truman's core despite the abundance of other furniture. Picking up his tea, therefore, he cradled its saucer in one hand while taking a sip from its cup with his other.

"I couldn't hide her away from the rest of the world; it wouldn't be proper," he said after the amber-coloured liquid had warmed his gullet. Looking across to his companion, he enquired, "But, have I done the right thing, Miss Trent?"

"Speaking as both a woman *and* the clerk of the Bow Street Society, I doubt such measures would've granted you peace of mind. In my opinion, it would've given your wife a greater compulsion to transgress—a natural reaction from any human when put into such a situation." Taking her notebook from the low table between them, Miss Trent opened it up at a clean page. "I presume she *has* transgressed in some way?"

Mr Truman put his cup and saucer down. "Yes."

"In that case, it's my duty to inform you the Bow Street Society is reluctant to become involved in domestic cases surrounding accusations of infidelity," Miss Trent explained.

Mr Truman looked up sharply. "Y—You are…?"

"Unless there is another—more unusual problem—to be resolved that has a direct bearing upon the accusation," Miss Trent said. "In those cases, the Society may investigate the problem on behalf of the client to assist with answering the question of infidelity."

Mr Truman absently scratched at his knees as his gaze dropped to Miss Trent's notebook. "I see…" Falling silent, he withdrew his hands to hold them within his lap. After a few moments of consideration, he continued, "…The question of my wife's infidelity does rest upon the legitimacy of a confession she's made to me." He met Miss Trent's gaze. "Not about her infidelity but an explanation for her unnatural behaviour."

Miss Trent held her pencil, poised, over her notebook. "If you could start from the very beginning, Mr Truman, I shall then make a decision regarding your case."

"Yes, of course." He smiled weakly. "It's always best to start a book at the beginning, isn't it?" When Miss Trent returned his smile, he retrieved his cup and saucer to take another sip of tea. "My wife Gloria and I were married a month ago. Our courtship was pleasant enough, and she seemed happy on our wedding day.

"In the days following our honeymoon, though, she became distant and quiet. She'd hardly eat or speak. I thought she might be sick—or with child—but she repeatedly spurned my calls to fetch the doctor." Mr Truman moved forward and returned his tepid tea to the tray. Remaining perched upon the sofa's edge, his back bent, he once again scratched his knees. "During our courtship, I was introduced to her brother, Mr Duncan Smethwick. Their parents live in the south but are in failing health. Her brother therefore took on her father's responsibilities as far as approving the marriage, and so forth. After we were wed, Mr Smethwick continued to visit, and would even stay overnight on occasion. Even in the beginning, it was clear how close a bond the siblings shared. Gloria would—quite simply—come alive whenever she was with him. It was as though he was the spark to her fire. When she became distant and less talkative with me, I was gladdened to see her malady hadn't extended to her brother. I ardently encouraged his visits as a result and, soon, he became a permanent resident—quite by accident, you understand."

"Does your wife and Mr Smethwick share chambers on occasion?"

"She may fall asleep while in the parlour with him but, up until a week ago, I would've insisted they'd never shared a bed."

"What happened a week ago?" Miss Trent enquired, making a note of what he'd already told her.

"We had enjoyed a fine dinner together, me, Gloria, and Mr Smethwick. Afterwards, he and I conversed about politics by the fire in the parlour, while Gloria did her needlework. At eleven o'clock, it was unanimously decided we would retire to bed; Gloria and I went to the master bedroom and Mr Smethwick to the guest bedroom on the other side of the house.

"As had become customary, my wife completed her night-time preparations with barely a word spoken to me. I was quite exhausted that night so I didn't press her. We went to bed and, within minutes, I was asleep. At around one-thirty in the morning, though, I was awoken by the sound of distant voices. Naturally, I turned over to address my wife but—to my surprise—I discovered her absent. I at once rose from bed, put on my robe, and went to look for her. First, I walked down the hall, toward the stairs. I had, on occasion, discovered her asleep in the parlour's armchair, so I thought this might be the case again.

"When I neared the stairs, however, I again heard the voices. Realising they were coming from the other hall, I followed their sound along the landing. Imagine my alarm, Miss Trent, when I not only heard them coming from Mr Smethwick's room but also how distressed Gloria was."

"Did you go inside?"

Mr Truman's features drooped and taking his handkerchief from his pocket, he pressed it against his nose and mouth a moment. With a curt shake of his head, he removed the handkerchief and admitted, "I was about to—I even reached for the door knob—but Gloria's words stayed my hand."

The stoicism dissolved from Miss Trent's gaze. "Please, take all the time you need, Mr Truman."

Taking a deep breath and giving a more confident nod, he replied, "Thank you." He looked to the crumpled handkerchief in his hands. "I fear the shock of what I overheard still runs through my veins." Tugging at the handkerchief's corners as he took a second, shuddering, breath, he then continued, "She said, 'It's no good, Duncan. He's bound to discover the truth, and where shall I be then?' To which I heard him reply, 'How shall he? We've kept it from him thus far. Besides, you know how worrying can affect you. Simply be yourself, and all will be well.' I know I should've thrown open the door and confronted them—despite the tremendous sickness raging in my belly—but I feared what I may see. To think I had ardently *encouraged* his presence in *my* home and all along they were *deceiving* me! I could not bear it. I strangled my gasp and rushed back to my room forthwith."

"And your wife…? Did she return that night?"

Mr Truman pressed his handkerchief against the corners of his eyes before stuffing it back into his pocket. "She did, around an hour later. I closed my eyes and she assumed me asleep. The next morning, she greeted me at breakfast with her usual smile, while *he* dared to read *my* newspaper, and remark upon its quality of journalism. At this, I lost my fear and gained my courage. I requested he leave my wife and me alone but, rather than doing as I had asked—as *any* man of sound reputation *should*—he questioned my reasoning. I was therefore forced to raise my voice—much to the clear distress of my wife—but this only made matters worse. He accused me of being disrespectful and vowed to protect his sister. I don't mind telling you, Miss Trent, I was *seething*."

Mr Truman stood and wandered around the room. With a hardened voice and expression, he continued, "I *commanded* he leave us, and threatened to have a constable fetched if he did not. At last—while my wife wept into her tea—he did as I asked and I was finally able to confront Gloria with what I'd overheard." He turned sharply upon his heel and, striding toward Miss Trent, bent forward and held up his cupped hands. "She *sobbed*, Miss Trent." Dropping back down onto the sofa with keen disquiet in his eyes and on his face, he continued, "Sobbed and begged for my forgiveness. Other men may have beat her for such a confession but I... I crumpled at her feet and wept into her knee. *All* I had held dear was *gone*!" He made a sweeping motion with his arm. "Swept away by those few words!" Holding his clenched hands in his lap, he cried, "And, yet, she *denied* it, Miss Trent! Even as she sobbed and begged for my forgiveness, she *denied* her brother was really her lover in disguise! Instead, she claimed her declining appetite, her distancing herself from my affection, and late-night discussions with Mr Smethwick were all due to her suffering from somnambulism!"

Miss Trent's brow lofted.

"*Sleepwalking,* Miss Trent," Mr Truman said. "She insisted she'd suffered with it since she was a child, but had kept it from me for fear of my refusing to marry her." He pressed his handkerchief against his eyes once more. "I didn't know *what* to believe then. I abandoned her in the breakfast room and locked myself away in my study. Since then, her appetite has declined further, and she flees the room whenever I enter. I could command her to stay and show respect to her husband, but I... I *love* her, Miss Trent. For all her deception, evasiveness, and coldness toward me, I worship her as much now as I did when we wed. So, you see, I *must* have the Bow Street Society's assistance. I must *know*, once and for all, if she is indeed a somnambulist or a scheming harlot."

Miss Trent closed her notebook and set aside her pencil. "It's clear how detrimental this whole affair has been to you, Mr Truman," she said, her tone and expression sombre in equal measure. "Given the nature of your problem, I would recommend you meet with our members here. If you've time to wait, therefore, I'll arrange for them come at once."

"Yes, absolutely," Mr Truman replied, pushing his handkerchief back into his pocket. "I'll abide by your advice."

II

The parlour door opened and a slender woman of around thirty years old entered. Behind her came a petite woman of eighteen followed by Miss Trent. The first was remarkably tall without the comparison of her associate. At six feet, she had at least two inches on Mr Truman. Her dark blue-green eyes peered down at him from beneath delicate brows which matched her dark-blonde, wavy hair. The latter was pinned up on her head's crown to create a sculpted style that continued to the nape of her neck. Soft cheekbones accentuated the smooth lines of her facial features, thereby intensifying her handsomeness. Her attire consisted of a pale-pink, loosely fitting blouse, a high-waist, dark-brown, straight-lined skirt, and a black belt with a brass buckle. Pinned to her bosom was a ceramic broach with a cluster of hand-painted, pink roses.

The second woman, though short, had perfect bodily proportions. Her flawless, fair skin was lightened further by the stark contrast with her auburn hair which she'd brushed back and tied into an understated, practical plait. Her attire comprised of a midnight-blue, high-necked, cotton dress with mutton chop-shaped sleeves and a black front panel on its straight-lined skirts. A wide, black band was also on her collar, between her breasts, and around her waist. While her taller associate met Mr Truman's gaze, she kept her green eyes upon his mouth and her slender hands clasped against her skirts.

Indicating the taller woman and then the shorter, Miss Trent introduced, "This is Doctor Lynette Locke, a fully qualified Doctor of Medicine, and Miss Georgina Dexter; a freelance artist. In addition to their usual employment, they're also members of the Bow Street Society. Given the circumstances of your case, Mr Truman, I've decided they are better suited to investigate. Doctor Locke, Miss Dexter, this is our client, Mr Warwick Truman. If you'd all care to take a seat." Miss Trent stood before the sofa's end closest to the door and, waiting until

Dr Locke and Miss Dexter had taken the remaining space and Mr Truman the armchair, continued, "Mr Truman, I've already informed Doctor Locke and Miss Dexter of what you told me earlier. I'm certain they'll have their own questions to ask you, however."

"I'll answer them as best as I can," Mr Truman replied, looking to the two women with a polite smile. "Please, whatever you can do to help me would be greatly appreciated."

"We shall do our utmost," Dr Locke replied, her voice professional in its tone. "There are a few points I'd like to clarify with you. Firstly, you told Miss Trent your wife claimed to suffer from somnambulism but had been frightened to tell you of it for fear of your withdrawing your proposal of marriage. During your courtship, had you ever given her cause to fear such a thing?"

"None whatsoever," Mr Truman replied, leaning forward in his chair. "As I told Miss Trent, I'm rather liberal in my treatment of Gloria."

"You had expressed sympathy toward Somnambulists in the past, then?" Dr Locke enquired, glancing at Miss Dexter who was listening to, and watching, Mr Truman in silence. Thus far, his reactions and body language appeared to be as expected.

"I may have done… I can't really say with confidence if I had or hadn't," he replied.

Dr Locke hummed, "Secondly, you told Miss Trent you'd occasionally find your wife, asleep, in the parlour during the night. Didn't you suspect it was a result of her somnambulism, once she'd confessed her condition to you?"

Mr Truman frowned, "I had considered it, yes. None of the servants have ever seen her sleepwalking, though. Nor have I, for that matter. She has never fallen down the stairs, or awoken with bruises, as you sometimes hear Somnambulists do. Then there is the matter of what I overheard—"

"Words which could, also, be referring to her sleepwalking," Dr Locke pointed out. "That being said, somnambulism is an easy condition to impersonate."

Mr Truman swallowed hard and, retrieving his handkerchief again, pulled it loose from its ball. He remarked, "And a simple explanation for her presence in Mr Smethwick's bedroom."

"Perhaps," Dr Locke replied. "True Somnambulists have certain traits which set them apart, however. If I can identify these traits in your wife, it will provide credence to her story."

"I'll also take photographs," Miss Dexter interjected. "With my box camera, so you may see them for yourself."

"To ensure our findings are accurate, though, I must urge you *not* to inform your wife of your visit to the Society today *or* of our involvement in your disagreement."

"I understand…" Mr Truman replied, folding and unfolding his handkerchief upon his knee while keeping his gaze on the two women. "…But how do you propose to gather your evidence? My wife only sleeps at night."

"Then we must be there when she does," Dr Locke said.

"Is Mr Smethwick still at your home, sir?" Miss Dexter enquired.

"Yes… I can't expel him without uncompromising evidence of my accusation. He's the sort of man who'd ensure I regret my actions," Mr Truman replied, his frown twisting into a grimace.

"His presence will serve our purpose well," Dr Locke said, prompting Mr Truman's eyes to narrow. Before he could protest though, Dr Locke added, "If your wife *is* deceiving you, and Mr Smethwick is her lover after all, she will call upon him during the night. She can't do that if he isn't there."

Mr Truman folded his handkerchief in half and, putting it back into his pocket, mumbled, "A rational argument, I suppose."

"I propose for Miss Dexter and me to visit your home at midnight tonight once the household is asleep," Dr Locke said, maintaining her stoic professionalism. "We shall hide ourselves where we have a clear view of both your bedroom door and the guest bedroom. If your wife is indeed a somnambulist, she should have a fit of her condition. In which case, Miss Dexter and I will put her to the test."

"Very well," Mr Truman replied, his fingers absently scratching at his knee once more. "Should I inform my servants of your arrival?"

Dr Locke and Miss Dexter exchanged glances, yet it was the former who replied, "We shall require someone else to let us into the house. You may awaken your wife if you leave your bed. Provided you may trust him, I would recommend taking your butler into your confidence."

"He's served me well all these years," Mr Truman replied. "Yes, I believe I can trust him."

"Excellent," Dr Locke said with a soft smile. "Until tonight, then."

III

In the coming hours, the weather in London deteriorated. The rainfall became torrential and violent winds descended from the north. Horses struggled to canter against the gales, while their cabs and carriages swayed and swerved under the force. Shivering passengers squeezed into the omnibuses' lower decks, and dockworkers fought to unload cargo from ships unscathed. By the time midnight arrived, the storm was at its full strength. Those with homes had deserted the streets, while those without were forced to find shelter wherever they could. The only figures Dr Locke and Miss Dexter saw from the Society's cab as it drove toward Mr Truman's street, therefore, were the desperate prostitutes and hardened constables. Even when the cab came to a halt outside their destination, the flames of the nearby gas lamps danced and shook at the wind's command.

Built in a fashion similar to most townhouses in the affluent areas of London, the Truman residence had iron railings on street level and a set of stone steps leading downward to a passageway and door. A much shorter set of steps led one from the pavement to a shallow portico with two broad pillars surmounted by a white stone pediment. Rain poured from the pediment's roof and struck the passageway's paved floor below. The tall windows on either side of the portico, denoting the ground floor rooms, were in darkness. A similar sight could be found in the three shorter windows on the floor above and the floor above that.

Dr Locke and Miss Dexter alighted from the cab and bid goodbye to its driver. With the sound of its wheels trundling against the cobblestones at their backs, the two Bow Streeters hurried through the railings' unlocked gate and down the steps to the passageway. As well as the door at its end, two windows overlooked the passageway. While the first was in darkness, the second had a lit kerosene lamp standing upon a table beyond its glass.

When Dr Locke and Miss Dexter reached it, they discovered a man of sixty years—attired in the white shirt and black waistcoat of a butler's uniform—sitting by the lamp. At their gentle knock upon the glass, he lifted his chin from his chest, adjusted his rounded spectacles, and squinted at them through the dim light. "Bow Street Society," Dr Locke mouthed to him. The butler lifted a hand and, getting to his feet, hurried from view.

Moments later, the Bow Streeters heard footsteps and a bolt being slid back beyond the door. A shaft of golden light then appeared, followed by the butler's grey eyes and white whiskers. Taking a moment to scrutinise their faces further, he pulled the door wide and ushered them inside.

"The master told me why you're 'ere," the butler said as he slid the bolt back into place.

The room they were standing in was revealed to be a narrow, windowless hall with a flagstone floor and whitewashed walls. It turned at a severe right angle, toward the house's rear, the moment one entered. Several doors—all closed—lined its righthand side. A narrow beam of light emitted from the first door—presumably the room where the butler had been seen in—but the remainder of the hall was in darkness. From a narrow shelf by the door, the butler took two brass candleholders, with shallow trays and rounded handles, which he gave to Dr Locke and Miss Dexter. Standing within their holders were two lit candles.

"If you follow this hall," the butler continued, pointing into the abyss. "You'll come to the back stairs. Go up one lot and you'll come to a door. Through there's the hallway. On your left's the main stairs, on your right's the main door. Go up the stairs and you'll come to the landing. The master's bedroom's down the hall on the left, first door you come to. Mr Smethwick's room's down the hall on the right, first door you come to." He shuffled around on the spot to face them. "There's no lamps on, 'cause the master told me not to. You'll need to be careful;

break something and you'll wake the whole house, not to say pay for it, too."

"We shall be as silent as the grave, Mr…?" Dr Locke said.

"Paterson," the butler replied.

Dr Locke smiled. "Your assistance is appreciated, Mr Paterson." Looking to Miss Dexter—who was hugging her box camera against her bosom with one hand and balancing the candleholder with her other—Dr Locke led the way down the hall. Unperturbed by the darkness, she had a fleeting thought about her husband encountering such situations while carrying out his own assignments for the Society. A smirk formed as she recalled his reaction to her evening's plans. Though he'd not said as much, his envy was palatable. *Not this time, darling*, she mused.

Miss Dexter, on the other hand, listened to her heart's rapid thump. Feeling lightheaded when they neared the back stairs, she released the breath she'd not been aware of holding. The creak of wood beneath their feet as they ascended stilled her for a moment. In the near silence, the small noise had sounded like an explosion. Listening to Dr Locke's continued climb, she waited for a voice or running, neither emerged. Slowly exhaling therefore, she hurried to catch up with her fellow Bow Streeter, finally doing so in the hallway described by Mr Paterson.

Though a vast space, the lack of light and thundering rain gave the room a claustrophobic atmosphere. Miss Dexter kept close to Dr Locke as a result, the rustling of their respective skirts masked by the loud ticking of a grandfather clock. They weaved their way around an oversized table, complete with wax floral arrangement, set in the hall's centre. A soft carpet—whose colour was lost in the darkness—muffled their footfalls as they ascended the main staircase.

When they were only halfway up, Dr Locke paused to blow out her candle and tapped Miss Dexter's arm for her to do the same. Miss Dexter bit her lip but, seeing their long shadows cast against the walls up ahead, relented. As soon as they were plunged into utter darkness, she felt her breathing quicken.

Gripping her camera all the tighter, she remained at Dr Locke's side until they reached the summit. The landing was deserted and quiet, much to her relief. Glancing around, she pointed to a spot behind them and Dr Locke nodded. Creeping along the landing to it, the two Bow Streeters then settled against the wall to watch the hallways Mr Paterson had pointed out. Miss Dexter, for one, was glad to be still for a while. Dr Locke was already checking the time upon her dainty pocket watch, however.

"What do we do if she doesn't leave her bedroom?" Miss Dexter whispered.

A loud click in the distance diverted her attention back to the hallways. Holding her breath, she glanced at Dr Locke but she, too, had her gaze fixed on the other side of the landing. Without a sound, a young woman in a white nightgown then emerged from the hallway on the left. She was barefoot, with her arms resting at her sides, as she shuffled toward the stairs.

In her early twenties, she had waist-length, brown hair which fell down in waves. Her slender form could be seen through the fabric of the loosely fitting nightgown on account of the moonlight pouring through the window at the hall's end. What Miss Dexter hadn't realised until now, though, was the fact the woman's eyes were closed! Lifting her box camera with trembling hands, Miss Dexter repeatedly pressed its button with several loud clicks. Though Miss Dexter had winced at each sound, no reaction came from the wandering woman.

Dr Locke watched with equal interest. Setting down her candleholder upon the floor, she crept toward the woman. While the latter reached the end of the hallway and stopped, Dr Locke paused at the corner of the landing and waited. Despite there being around ten feet between them, the woman's eyes remained closed and her steady breathing didn't alter. After a few moments, her shuffle resumed and she turned right to walk along the landing toward the other hallway. When she passed, Dr Locke swept her hand past the woman's face but, still, there was no reaction.

"Shouldn't we wake her?" Miss Dexter whispered as she joined her fellow Bow Streeter.

"Not yet," Dr Locke replied. When the woman passed the hallway and turned right, though, Dr Locke's brow lofted. "Where is she going…" she muttered. Picking up her skirts, she went along the landing with Miss Dexter at her back. The two came to an abrupt halt a few feet away, however, when the woman opened a door and ascended a staircase. "Did Mr Paterson mention those stairs?"

Miss Dexter shook her head.

"Then we must hurry," Dr Locke replied, breaking into a jog to reach the concealed stairs in a matter of moments. Pausing to look up, she saw the train of the woman's nightgown disappear around a corner at their top. "Come on," she hissed, pulling Miss Dexter by the arm and taking the stairs two at a time. At the top, they found a long, narrow room with tall windows lining the left side and numerous large pieces of furniture covered by sheets. While the rain pounded against glass, and the wind howled through the frames, a single figure in white reached to open the central window.

"Wait!" Dr Locke cried.

A heartbeat later, a barrage of wind and rain erupted into the room. The sheets' sides flapped incessantly, the wind's howls became louder, and the rain soaked everything in sight—including Dr Locke and Miss Dexter. Yet, despite the tempest, the woman remained standing at the opened window, her hands holding both sides. Her hair was whipped around in all directions, while her nightgown became stuck to her slim body from the rain drenching its fabric.

"Mrs Truman!" Dr Locke yelled over the noise. Holding up her bent arm to shield her eyes, she moved toward the woman. "Mrs Truman, *no!*" she yelled upon seeing her step up onto the window ledge. Lunging toward her, Dr Locke threw out her arms and wrapped them around her waist just as she toppled through the window. As the woman's weight threatened to take Dr Locke with her, the latter wedged her feet against the wall beneath the ledge. Forcing her shoulders back, while straightening her legs, she attempted to throw herself against the floor as hard as she could.

"Doctor Locke!" Miss Dexter cried as she, too, rushed to the window, reaching it in time to see the two ladies dropping onto the floor. "Doctor Locke," she repeated, slamming the window shut and offering her hand. "Are you hurt?"

"Where am I?!" the brown-haired woman suddenly cried, her eyes wide open and darting around frantically. "Wh—why am I wet?!"

Dr Locke sat up and, taking the offered hand, got to her feet. "I'm fine," she reassured, reaching down to help Mrs Truman to stand with Miss Dexter's assistance. "You were sleepwalking, Mrs Truman," she said and removed her coat to drape it around the shivering woman's shoulders. "Let us get you downstairs where Mr Paterson can make you some sweet tea." Though still shaken, Mrs Truman gave a disjointed nod and allowed them to lead her to the warmth and safety of the butler's parlour.

IV

"It's true, then," Mr Truman said. Standing before the tremendous fireplace in his parlour, he swallowed some brandy and turned toward the others. While he was in his nightwear and robe, his wife had changed into a dry nightgown with a woollen blanket wrapped around her shoulders. She sat in an armchair to the left of the fire, and Dr Locke and Miss Dexter stood at her sides. They, too, were wrapped in blankets but their hair and clothes remained soggy. All three ladies cradled steaming cups of tea in their hands while they looked upon Mr Truman.

"It is..." Mrs Truman replied, her voice hoarse from the cold and damp. Her timid eyes couldn't hold their gaze upon her husband's for more than a few seconds before breaking away. "I am so very sorry, Warwick."

"From what Miss Dexter and I witnessed," Dr Locke began. "And what you shall witness for yourself, Mr Truman, once Miss Dexter's photographs have been developed, I am confident your wife is a true somnambulist. While recovering from her ordeal, your wife explained how her brother, Mr Smethwick, has known about her condition for years. He has assisted her in keeping it a secret because he—like her—feared she would lose your love."

"That would *never* happen, my darling," Mr Truman said, moving to kneel at his wife's feet. Placing his hands upon hers, he looked into her eyes, "I *love* you. I would exchange all the riches in the world to see you smile for me again."

"Oh, *Warwick*..." Mrs Truman said, breaking down into sobs as she put her arm around him and buried her face into his shoulder. "I love you, too! So very, very much."

"We thought it best not to rouse Mr Smethwick from his own slumber," Dr Locke said. "You both need time to come to terms with what has happened, so you may explain to him come dawn. In the meantime, I would suggest making plans to take the waters at Bath, or to some fresh air on the south coast. Your wife's worrying over your potential reaction could have played a substantial part in the frequency of her somnambulism—*and* the dream that led to her attempt at leaping from a window."

"I've been such a *fool*!" Mr Truman cried, holding his wife tight. "I shall take you away, my darling. We shall spend time together—*happy* time together. I promise you," he held her face in his hands as he looked into her eyes. "I *promise* you."

The Case of the Chilling Chamber

I

A breath of air brushed against the fair complexion of a young woman's cheek as she sat by an open sash window. Disharmonious sounds of wagon wheels over cobblestones, clip-clopping hooves, and imperceptible conversations from Bow Street assaulted her hearing. At the same time, a bouquet of odours—specifically, stale sweat and smoke—conquered her sense of smell. Dark-brown eyes regarded their origin—a male sat opposite—with disdain for the briefest of moments. She subtly angled her nose toward the window and breathed through her parted lips.

He was in his mid-forties, of stout build, and close to six feet in height. Damp patches soiled his shirt's underarms, while twisted, mousey-brown strands of hair clung to his pallid forehead like rats' tails. A bloated neck and bulbous nose, framed by swollen cheeks and beady, grey-green eyes, further strengthened the impression of an ogre's countenance. Dried mud clung to his trousers and boots, the latter of which having trod a trail of dust into the parlour. The young woman glanced at the offensive footprints with a thought to sweep them away later.

Unlike his, her attire was devoid of contaminates. A sunshine-yellow, cotton dress followed the natural curve of her waist and hung down, loose, in straight-lined skirts to her ankles. Its gathered sleeves ended below her shoulders, while the high-edged, sweetheart neckline preserved her modesty. Intricate rose and leaf reliefs were embroidered into the skirts' top layer of pastel-yellow lace. Handmade, white-cotton roses were also nestled amongst her chestnut-brown hair's tight curls, which were arranged into a sculptured mass atop her head's crown.

The parlour, in which the two sat, had a high ceiling, wide-chimney fireplace, and a door opening onto a vast hallway. All of which served to maintain a cool atmosphere despite the intense heat and humidity outside. Aside from the high-backed kitchen chairs they sat on, the parlour's furniture consisted of a sofa, armchair, low table, and bookcase. Almost all available surface space was covered by trinkets, ornaments, or books. Even the walls were speckled with framed prints of floral bouquets or scenic countryside. There were no familial portraits, however.

"My name is Miss Rebecca Trent, the Bow Street Society's clerk, and the one responsible for accepting commissions on its behalf."

"Oh, right." The man's accent was an odd mixture of London's East End and Scotland's Edinburgh. "I woz expectin' a bloke—like Sherlock Holmes, y'know?"

Miss Trent gave a contrived smile. "How may we be of service, Mr...?"

"Glenn Toller. You'll prob'ly laugh at what I've got to say, but I've not come 'ere to be a nuisance. I've got nowt else if the Society won't do for me. The Missus says I should get a vicar in, but what's 'e gonna do, I ask?"

Miss Trent retrieved her notebook and pencil from the windowsill. "If you could start from the beginning, Mr Toller, I can then make a decision as to whether or not it would be useful for the Society to look into the matter." When Mr Toller shifted in his chair to dip and scratch his head, she reassured, "Many people have come here before you, each as reluctant as you to tell me their story. Yet, the Bow Street Society originated to help people who aren't able to get it from the police—for various reasons. Even if your problem isn't suitable for us to investigate, Mr Toller, I can assure you I shan't mock you for it."

Mr Toller lifted his head and gave a weak smile. "That's very good of you, Miss Trent…" His gaze shifted toward the window as he continued, "I've been a publican for over ten years, but come by *The Rose and Thistle* last month. I'd lost my place b'fore that. The old bloke, what had *The Rose* at the time, was on his last legs. I had a bit put by, so I took the pub on.

"All was well 'til last week…" Mr Toller frowned. "Day started as any other. 'Round lunch time, we heard this *terrible* cry, like someone bein' taken by the Devil. Then, a splash. Everyone ran out, to the bankside, and saw this bloke floatin', belly down, in the water. 'Is head was right back though, touchin' 'is back b'tween 'is shoulders. Must've fallen, we thought, or murdered 'isself, from the window. Not that I'd seen out from 'im to say 'e'd do such a thing when he took the room that mornin'. Told me 'e woz a merchant seaman b'tween boats. Still, I thought, there's nowt as strange as folk and set to gettin' 'im fished out and 'is belongin's took to the constable."

"Mr Toller, I must inform you the Bow Street Society is reluctant to become involved with cases of suicide. When those left behind are unable to accept their loved one would carry out such an act, there's very little we can do to put their mind at ease—unless there's some suspicion of foul play—"

"There might well be, 'cause of the window."

"What of it?"

"It don't open."

Miss Trent stared at him a moment. "I beg your pardon, but I think I misheard you. Did you say the window he fell, or leapt, from doesn't open…?"

"Hasn't for years, or so I'm told."

"And you're certain he came from *that* window?"

"That woz 'is room, Miss Trent, and there's no more windows on that side."

Miss Trent considered the problem. After several moments—and prolonged scrutiny of his facial features for hints of deception—she straightened and took a deep breath. "It's certainly perplexing—impossible, even, on the face of it." She turned the page in her notebook, "I will arrange for some of our members to call upon *The Rose and Thistle* this afternoon, Mr Toller."

"That's very good of you, Miss Trent, only…money's short right now and—"

"We'll investigate your case free of charge; it's certainly intriguing enough to warrant it. If I may have the address, then?"

"*Oh*, thank you, yes, it's just up from the *Phoenix Gas Works* and Blackfriars' Bridge."

Miss Trent closed her notebook and set it aside. "Excellent." She rose to her feet. "Goodbye, Mr Toller."

II

"*The Rose and Thistle's* on the bank of the Thames," Mr Samuel Snyder began in his rough, East End of London-accented voice. His stubby finger tapped the map laid out upon Miss Trent's kitchen table. "There, by the Alms Houses on Pond Road, west of the Globe and Stone wharfs." His finger slid across the map and tapped it, again. "Gas Works are 'ere."

He folded his broad, hairy arms and rested them upon his extended stomach, his larger-than-average hands tucked beneath each elbow. A dark-red neckerchief peeked out from under a white shirt, whose top button was undone and its sleeves rolled up. In his late-forties—and thus one of the Bow Street Society's oldest members—he'd spent many years as a hansom cab driver. Consequentially, his facial skin was weathered and his fingers calloused. Thick, black, bushy sideburns adorned his jawline, while his head hair was the same colour and just as unkempt due to sweat. His brown, beady eyes peered out from beneath dense eyebrows at Miss Trent.

"It's quite the journey, then," Mr Bertram Heath remarked to Mr Snyder's left, however. He—despite being halfway to thirty—possessed the countenance of someone much younger. This was wholly down to the delicate angles of his facial features and large eyes. In contrast to Mr Snyder, his own, light-brown hair was combed, while his jaw and upper lip were clean shaven. Furthermore, his enunciation was more succinct, partly due to his profession as an architect and partly due to his being an associate of the Royal Institute of Architects. Born in Portsmouth, he'd often marvelled at how formal his accent had become.

"It's not a good idea to take the cab," Mr Snyder

replied. "'Cause the streets 'round the pub ain't what you'd call friendly to toffs." He paused to glance at Mr Heath and then at Mr Maxwell—the latter, in Mr Snyder's opinion, passing as a gentleman by a small margin.

A journalist with the *Gaslight Gazette*, Mr Joseph Maxwell was younger than all of them at twenty-one. Unlike his fellow Bow Streeters, though, his complexion lacked any vibrancy. Instead, it was pale to the point of being ghost-like. The abundance of freckles—which were strewn across his high cheekbones—did little to ease this impression. Neither did the dark shade of his auburn eyelashes and eyebrows. His wavy hair—though the same colour as his brows—looked all the darker against his pale face. When Mr Snyder looked at him, Mr Maxwell swallowed the lump in his throat and wiped his sweaty palms upon his dark-green frockcoat's skirt. Despite the day's humidity, his remaining attire consisted of a black, cotton waistcoat, long-sleeved, white shirt, dark-green, silk cravat, and trousers. Needless to say, he regretted his decision.

"What would you suggest, then, Mr Snyder?" Mr Heath enquired.

"You two've got to wear sumin' old and meet me back 'ere," Mr Snyder replied. "Then, we walk down Wellington Street 'til we get to the Waterloo Pier, where we'll get on the steamer and take it to the pier at Blackfriars'." Mr Snyder pointed out a small pier on the map. It was nestled between the two thoroughfares which made up Blackfriars' Bridge, the left for horse-drawn vehicles and pedestrians, the right for steam locomotives. "Steps up'll take us to the bridge. We cross that on foot, then down 'ere onto the bankside, and then along it 'til we get to the pub. To come back, we can get the steamer, or walk to the cabman shelter near St. Clement Danes."

"The steamer would be the most logical option," Mr Heath remarked as he slipped a hardboiled sweet into his mouth.

"Yeah, but we'll see 'ow you two fare on the water," Mr Snyder replied with a smirk as he looked to Mr Maxwell once more.

"P-pardon me," Mr Maxwell began, framing his Adam's apple with his thumb and index finger, as he, instead, addressed Miss Trent. "But… why do I have to go along? I-I understand Mr Heath and Mr Snyder's involvement b-but I'm unclear as to wh-what you expect *me* to do…"

"There may have been other deaths, associated with the window, prior to the one last week," Miss Trent replied. "I therefore think it would be wise for you to search the *Gaslight Gazette's* archives for such."

"Y-Yes, I had assumed as much, but… why am I required to visit the pub?" Mr Maxwell enquired.

Miss Trent placed a hand upon her hip as she pursed her lips together. After a moment, she said, "You're a journalist, Mr Maxwell. Use that expertise to find out as much as possible from the pub's customers."

Mr Snyder chuckled. "Best to wear sumin' *really* old, then, Mr Maxwell. You don't wanna know what they'd do to you otherwise."

Mr Maxwell's eyes widened. At the same time, large beads of sweat also formed upon his face and his complexion turned a shade paler. "P-Pardon…?"

Mr Snyder chuckled for a second time and, giving Mr Maxwell's back a solid pat, replied, "Mind my words and all will be well."

Mr Maxwell gave a soft grunt as the large hand jerked his body forward. "I-I will…"

III

A shrill whistle crossed the bridge as—with a rhythmic *chooga-chooga*, rumble of wheels, and trail of sulphurous smoke—the next expected steam locomotive approached Blackfriars station. At the same time, the passenger steamer on its return journey from Chelsea chuffed its way beneath the bridge following its stop at St. Paul's Pier. Innumerable industrial barges also navigated their way along the "silent highway," destined for the warehouses and works which lined the River Thames. Each piece of available space along the riverbank had been choked by wharfs, soot-covered buildings, and unidentifiable pollution. Across the chaotic swell of brick, mortar, and tile—that sprawled out as far as the eye could see—were the thick, black plumes of domestic chimney smoke. With little wind to displace it, it had steadily sunk to ground level over the course of the morning. Thus, by the time the Bow Streeters reached *The Rose and Thistle*, a light smog had formed to clog the lungs and sting the eyes.

Overlooking the riverbank, *The Rose and Thistle* comprised of a three-storey building with awkward angles and crooked additions. Its central construction had whitewashed, plaster walls—irrevocably stained into a faecal brown with smeared edges—framed by rotten, warped, dark-oak beams. On its left side, when approaching from the riverbank, was Hind Alley, while, on its right, a narrow street led to Skin Yard. Yet, both routes led to an area of deplorable, abject poverty and vicious semi-criminality. The pub's main door was on the corner of Hind Alley. To the door's right was a rotund, lead-latticed window whose panes were smeared with soot dust and grime from the river.

Three sash windows lined the first and second floors of the pub's central structure. If one were to follow Hind Alley, one would find the pub's external wall to slope inwards until it came to a tall, wooden gate—presumably to a yard. Further along from the gate was the first row of dilapidated housings. Each of its doors had a crowd of dirty-faced women and children loitering around it, no doubt to escape the mould-riddled humidity of indoors.

Mr Maxwell held a handkerchief to his mouth as he followed Mr Snyder into the pub. His complexion had turned ashen, while his ink-stained fingers trembled. "I-I have never…" He swallowed the bile that threatened to erupt from his lips. "…In all my life. I'd like to request we… don't take the steamer back."

"I feel quite well," Mr Heath replied. "Pear drop?" He took the paper bag from his oversized, dark-brown coat and presented it to Mr Maxwell.

"No… thank you…" Mr Maxwell replied with a polite smile.

As instructed by Mr Snyder, Mr Maxwell and Mr Heath had dressed in the oldest clothes they had: Mr Maxwell in a moth-eaten, dark-blue suit he'd been about to dispose of, and Mr Heath in a faded, white shirt, black cravat tied as a neckerchief, and thread-bare trousers. Despite their efforts, though, their arrival was met with stifled conversations and suspicious glares. Unperturbed by the reception, Mr Snyder approached the narrow bar to address the man behind. Mr Maxwell and Mr Heath, meanwhile, followed at such close proximity, the former tripped on Mr Snyder's heels and almost toppled into the bar.

"I'm Sam Snyder, this 'ere's Bert Heath and Joe Maxwell. We're from the Bow Street Society, 'ere to see a Glenn Toller. That you?"

The barman wiped a hairy arm under his nose, across his forehead, and, finally, upon a stained apron around his waist. "Yeah, that's me." He offered his hand to Mr Snyder, who shook it without hesitation. When it was next offered to Messiers Heath and Maxwell, though, the two exchanged nervous glances.

"Mr Toller…" Mr Heath said, taking the soiled hand to give it a brief shake. Mr Maxwell wasn't so forthcoming, however.

"Shake 'is 'and, Joe…" Mr Snyder urged, his rough voice made all the more so by its low volume.

Mr Maxwell cleared his throat and, with an upward curl of his lips, slipped his slender hand into Mr Toller's moist palm. "P-Pleasure… sir…"

"You, too," Mr Toller replied, releasing his hand.

"Bert's an architect," Mr Snyder continued, while Mr Maxwell stepped behind him to wipe his hand with a handkerchief. "'E's come to look at the window."

"Yes." Mr Heath offered a warm smile. "I understand someone fell from it last week, but it doesn't open…?"

Mr Toller tensed and glanced around at his regulars' suspicious glares. "Not so loud, yeah?" He moved out from behind the bar, "Tarina, look after this 'til I come back down."

A woman in her thirties, with wiry, brown hair and deep-set, brown eyes, nodded.

"This way," Mr Toller continued as he led the three Bow Streeters through the dimly lit, densely occupied room. Sawdust, soiled by dropped ale and dirt, stuck to their boots as they went. Few of the drinkers moved aside, too. Thus compelling the group to separate and reform several times before they reached the stairs. When they did climb them, the weakened wood creaked beneath them.

"Room's down 'ere," Mr Toller said, his shoulders brushing the walls of the low-ceilinged, second floor corridor as he walked through it. The floor peaked and trothed under foot when the others followed. Halfway along, Mr Heath crouched and ran the flats of his hands over the dark-oak boards. Next, he turned upon his heels and traced the joins between the floor and wall. Repeating this inspection on the other side, he hummed and rose to his feet. Messiers Toller, Snyder, and Maxwell gathered at an open doorway at the end of the corridor, watching him with interest.

"I see the oak in your floor has warped over the years," Mr Heath remarked when he'd joined them. "Pardon me." He sidestepped through the doorway and cast a glance over the room beyond. He then crouched to inspect the floor with his hands. "As I expected…"

"It's an old place," Mr Toller said.

"Indeed!" Mr Heath said with a smile as he straightened and wiped the dirt from his hands. "It's an example of the typically Tudor style of around 1550-1558, I believe. The bay window downstairs, this half-timber work you can see all around…" He gestured toward the walls and the ceiling. "All evidence of this." He strolled around the sparsely furnished bedroom—an iron, double bed, stout wardrobe, and wash stand were all he could see at first glance. "This *particular* architectural style is known for its tendency to impose decorative elements from the Renaissance onto the perpendicular gothic style. I was surprised not to see patterned brickwork or elaborate carvings. Though, as you say, it's an old building and one, I suspect, has been altered, damaged, and rebuilt over time. Its proximity to the Thames no doubt causes problems from flooding in the winter…?"

"Yeah…" Mr Toller agreed. Having entered the room behind Mr Heath, he stood to the left of the door and folded his arms across his chest. Mr Snyder mimicked him in his actions, while Mr Maxwell kept close to the corridor.

"Has it always been known as *The Rose and Thistle*?" Mr Maxwell enquired as he took out a notebook and pencil.

"It was *The Highwayman* b'fore I come by it," Mr Toller replied. "Dunno 'bout b'fore then."

Mr Maxwell grasped his notebook close to his chest as he wrote down the name. "And the name of *The Highwayman's* publican?"

"Bob Dunn," Mr Toller replied.

"The warping of the floorboards is more severe in here," Mr Heath remarked. "The consequential impression it can leave on a man is one of disorientation; the lack of straight lines and stable perspective has been known to have this effect."

"That enough to make someone murder 'isself?'" Mr Toller enquired.

"I wouldn't know, I'm not a doctor." Mr Heath walked a little further into the room. "This is *the* window, I presume?" He indicated a long window—vertically rectangular in shape—housed within a brown-brick, square alcove. The window itself had diamond-shaped panes—held in place by lead latticing—housed within a wrought-iron frame. A long, sturdy handle was rusted to a loop attached to the frame. A dark-oak bench around ten inches deep, two feet long, and a foot wide was wedged between the alcove's walls beneath the window. The space between it and the floor was around a half foot.

At Mr Toller's nod, Mr Heath approached the alcove and felt his foot slip when he placed it beneath the bench. Retracting his appendage, therefore, he knelt on the floor and ran his hands underneath. With another hum, he stood and gripped the alcove's corners while kneeling on the bench to peer through the window. The River Thames dominated the view. Yet, even as he leaned forward and extended his neck to look downward, Mr Heath couldn't see below the alcove's external brickwork. An inspection of the handle revealed it to be immobile, while the window frame itself was attached to the internal brickwork.

"Has this window always been here, Mr Toller?" Mr Heath enquired as he stepped down from the bench, took another step back with his second foot, and turned toward the others.

"As far as I've been 'ere, yeah," Mr Toller replied.

"You couldn't guess as to when it was constructed, then?" Mr Heath enquired.

"No," Mr Toller replied. "Is that important?"

"I believe it may be," Mr Heath said. Running his eyes over the alcove, he remarked, "Doesn't its shape remind you of something, Mr Maxwell?"

"Erm…" Mr Maxwell swallowed and wiped his sweaty palms upon the skirt of his frockcoat. "N-Not really, I'm afraid… It just looks like a window to me."

"And me," Mr Toller replied.

"A *chimney*, gentlemen," Mr Heath said with an air of triumph. "A *chimney*. Its dimensions would suit a chimney *perfectly*. Mr Toller, would it be at all possible to see the window from the outside?"

"Only by boat," Mr Toller replied. "Way the pub's built, you can't see it from the road."

"Do you have a boat, then?" Mr Snyder enquired. At Mr Toller's nod, he added, "I'll row it, then. Joe, you stay 'ere."

Mr Maxwell breathed a sigh of relief and, lowering his notebook and pencil, said, "Y-Yes… th-thank you, Mr Snyder." He had felt his stomach lurch the moment *another* boat trip was proposed. The river's stench, during the journey there, was overpowering. He swallowed some more bile and slipped his notebook and pencil into his pockets. "I… I'll wait for you here."

"As you wish," Mr Heath replied and went to the door to leave. Turning sharply, though, he pointed to the window and warned, "But, under *no* circumstances must you approach the window. Do you understand?"

Mr Maxwell's eyes widened and he stared at him a moment. "H-have you found something, then…?"

"I believe so, but I must see the outside to be certain," Mr Heath replied. "I beg of you, then, *stay* by *this* door."

"I-I will," Mr Maxwell replied and followed them as far as the door. When they were out of sight, he returned to the room and pushed down upon the bed with his hand. It complained with a creak. He therefore decided against sitting on it.

The sudden shrill of a train's whistle in the distance then yanked a gasp from him and, with a racing heart, he stood with one hand on the bedframe and the other holding his chest. "The sooner we may leave this place the better…" he mumbled. The recollection of the steamer journey at once forced its way into his mind and he felt his stomach turn. "By train… definitely by train… or cab…"

He turned around on the spot, taking in his meagre surroundings with a mixture of trepidation, adrenaline, and impatience. From below, he heard the deep din of many voices, while the dry, dust-filled air irritated his throat and eyes.

"There it is, Mr Snyder!" Mr Heath's voice shouted outside.

Without further thought, Mr Maxwell strode toward the window with the intention of looking out. No sooner had he neared it, though, did he feel the floor give way beneath his feet and his body started to plummet.

"*Argh*!" He threw out his arms and, with a strangled grunt, struck the bench with his elbows while his feet flailed wildly. "*Help*!"

"Mr Maxwell?!" Mr Heath cried, having seen a trapdoor slam against the external brickwork, followed by his fellow Bow Streeter's legs. "I *warned* you to stay away from the window!"

"*Help* me, *please*!" Mr Maxwell screeched as the toes of his shoes scraped against the weathered bricks.

"We're comin'!" Mr Snyder shouted back and, turning the boat, rowed it toward the high—but muddy— riverbank beneath the trapdoor. From outside, he and Mr Heath had seen the window's alcove stopped abruptly. Rather than being a solid, cubed structure, therefore, it was a single wall of bricks built into the side of the building. The alcove itself, meanwhile, jutted out across the murky waters of the River Thames. "Hold on!"

"I don't know that I can!" Mr Maxwell cried as he felt his elbows start to slip on the bench's varnished wood. "Please, *hurry*—!" All of a sudden, he lost his grip and plummeted into the river with a tremendous splash.

"Mr Maxwell!" Mr Heath cried, his eyes wide.

Mr Snyder, on the other hand, was on his feet in

an instant. Without a moment's hesitation, he dove, head first, into the polluted water, swam to where Mr Maxwell had disappeared, and dove beneath the water's surface.

Mr Heath watched, and waited, from the safety of the row boat with baited breath. Several moments went by, but he saw no sign of his friends. Then, just as he was about to holler for help, Mr Snyder burst through the water's surface, a gasping Mr Maxwell clutched, tightly to him with a broad, hairy arm. "Thank *goodness!*" Mr Heath cried as he dropped down into the boat. "Well *done*, Mr Snyder! *Well* done!"

*   *   *

"Publican of *The Highwayman* tavern, Mr Harald Poole, was found guilty of multiple murders at the central criminal court in the Old Bailey this afternoon. The tavern, located on the banks of the River Thames near to Blackfriars Bridge, was found to contain a chute from a guest bedroom on the second floor to the kitchens in the cellar. The chute, crudely fashioned from a former chimney breast, had a trapdoor at its top," Mr Maxwell read aloud. Sensing eyes upon him, he lifted his gaze from the old edition of the *Gaslight Gazette* and saw many of *The Rose and Thistle's* customers both watching and listening to him. The atmosphere was different from that on the day prior; his swim in the Thames may have sparked some feelings of sympathy, perhaps? Clearing his throat, he shifted his gaze to those around his table—Mr Snyder, Mr Toller, and Mr Heath—and continued, "Mr Poole's unsuspecting victims were all guests who'd stepped onto the trapdoor—while standing at the window—and fell to their deaths.

"Mr Poole's hideous crimes were exposed following the discovery of a human skull among the animal bones on the river's bankside. Many of his victims' possessions—including silk handkerchiefs, gold and silver pocket watches, and jewellery—were found, hidden in a tin box, behind the tavern's stove when a search was conducted by Inspector John Conway of Scotland Yard." Mr Maxwell closed the *Gaslight Gazette* newspaper, "dated 19th April 1896, three months ago. Mr Poole was hung at Newgate Jail the next day."

"We can only assume, Mr Toller," Mr Heath began, "the publican before you, Mr Dunn, knew of the trapdoor. Unfortunately, he failed to notify you of its existence."

"Prob'ly thought you knew already," Mr Snyder remarked.

Mr Toller's face was ashen. "No, I…" He ran a grubby hand over his dirty hair. "…It's been blocked up, now… But… if it's always been there, why's more people not fell through it?"

"The warping of the floorboards," Mr Heath replied. Taking a sip of the lemonade their client had so graciously provided for them, he dabbed at his lips with his handkerchief and continued, "I mistook the sloping of the trapdoor—as it opened—as the floorboards being warped. It wasn't until I knelt on the floor and reached under the bench that I realised the truth. If others made the same mistake as I, they would've knelt upon the bench without stepping beneath it."

"But why have the bench there at all?" Mr Maxwell enquired.

"Break their necks on the way down, I think," Mr Snyder said. "Make sure they woz dead."

"Oh…" Mr Maxwell replied, holding his neck as he felt his stomach lurch. "Please… excuse me a moment…" He rose to his feet and, stepping around Mr Heath's chair, left the pub. A moment later, they heard violent retching and the three men looked toward the door.

"Oh *dear*," Mr Heath said with a frown. "*Poor* Mr Maxwell. It's a small miracle neither of you caught some *awful* pestilence from those waters. Perhaps I should go to him?"

"Nah," Mr Snyder replied as he lifted his pint of ale to his lips. "Best let 'im get it all out now." He drank a mouthful of ale and, setting the glass back down, added, with a smirk, "We've still gotta take the steamer back to Waterloo Pier, yet."

The Case of the Ghastly Gallop

I

"Mrrghh." Mr Xavior Ingham grimaced and set down his cup. "What ghastly concoction was that?" He held a clenched fist close to his lips and coughed, as he peered over his brass-rimmed pince-nez at the man sat opposite.

"Porter," Mr Callahan Skinner replied in a soft Dublin accent. The tin hip flask he'd poured the thin, black fluid from was returned to the inside pocket of his charcoal-coloured tail coat. "Good for what ails you."

"I would've preferred some brandy," Mr Ingham retorted. A man in his mid-twenties with drooping, hazel eyes, Mr Ingham's appearance often caused initial boredom in those he met. His protruding brow, high forehead, and underwhelming attire of someone beyond his years served to reinforce these assumptions regarding his character. Yet, the moment he spoke, those around him were encapsulated by his assertive tone, dynamic vocabulary, and impressive intellect.

In contrast, Mr Skinner was in his late thirties and had burn scars covering the right side of his jaw and cheek. Though short in height, he had broad shoulders and tremendous biceps. His brown hair—flecked with grey— was cut close to his head, while his posture was perfect. The cut and material of his trousers, riding boots, and coat were all of a high quality.

"We have none, unfortunately," Miss Trent replied. Sitting at the head of the table in the Bow Street Society's kitchen, she glanced at the well-developed bruise around Mr Ingham's left eye. "Mr Callahan Skinner is a member of the Society, here at my invitation to investigate the matter you spoke of on the telephone. He's a former officer with Her Majesty's Royal Navy. Thus, his knowledge of firearms, and other weaponry, is second to none." She referred to her notes. "Dr Rupert Alexander, a veterinary surgeon, will also be arriving soon." Several firm knocks sounded from the hallway. "There he is now. Excuse me a moment, please."

She left the kitchen with a rustle of her many, burgundy-coloured, cotton skirts. They were part of a long-sleeved dress with a square neckline framed by minute, hand-stitched, silk roses. A sash, pinned to her left hip with a silver brooch, ran across the front of her waist and ended where a second, silver brooch kept the skirts' top layer pinned to one side. Beneath, an embroidered panel of red roses—outlined in silver thread—added a sense of drama to the otherwise respectable dress. Her shoulder-length, chestnut-brown hair was styled into innumerable corkscrew ringlets, with only those around her face pinned back.

The men sat in silence while they awaited Miss Trent's return. Mr Ingham's gaze drifted over Mr Skinner's right hand. It rested upon the table but, unlike its counterpart, was swollen. Its fingers were rigid, too. Both appendages were covered by thick, brown, leather gloves but, as they heard the rustle of Miss Trent's skirts, Mr Skinner dragged his right hand from the table and deposited it upon his knee underneath.

"Allow me to introduce Dr Rupert Alexander," Miss Trent announced when she returned. Behind her came a man in his late-thirties with wavy, short, black hair parted at the side. Straight, thick, black brows capped his chestnut-brown eyes, while his most distinguishing features were his large, jutting-out ears and pointed nose. His attire consisted of a fastened, double-breasted, dark-green, cotton jacket over a cream-coloured shirt, with a plain, black bowtie and trousers. "Dr Alexander, this is Mr Xavior Ingham—the Bow Street Society's newest client. He's a partner of Mortimer & Ingham Insurance Broker's. Mr Callahan Skinner is another Society member I've assigned to Mr Ingham's case."

"A pleasure to meet you, Doctor," Mr Ingham said as he stood and extended his hand.

"The feeling is mutual, Mr Ingham," Dr Alexander replied with a hint of an Edinburgh accent.

Mr Skinner, who'd also risen, rested his right hand against his stomach and offered his left to Dr Alexander next. "Doctor."

"Mr Skinner." Dr Alexander smiled. "I don't believe I've ever had the pleasure of your acquaintance."

"This is the first time you'll be working together. Mr Skinner is a former officer with Her Majesty's Royal Navy, and now serves as Lady Mirrell's personal bodyguard," Miss Trent interjected. "Please, sit, gentlemen."

Dr Alexander's gaze drifted over Mr Skinner's scarred face. Yet, his next remark was to Mr Ingham. "My, that's a fine-looking bruise you have, sir."

"Indeed," Mr Ingham replied. "Courtesy of Mr Diarmaid Duffy, head groomsman at Lord Castleridge's estate."

"A nasty piece of work, if you don't mind my sayin'," Mr Skinner remarked.

"You know of him?" Mr Ingham enquired, intrigued.

"Aye." Mr Skinner lifted his swollen hand a couple of inches off the table. "Please, go on wit your story."

Mr Ingham frowned but, with a clearing of his throat, used his handkerchief to polish his pince-nez. "It's a claim on an insurance policy—by Lord Castleridge—that took me to his estate this afternoon. A retired racehorse of his—Cunning Tom—was insured for £5,000. His value based partly upon the potential revenue generated by his being a stud horse, you understand." Mr Ingham returned his pince-nez to his nose. "Lord Castleridge contacted my firm, announcing Cunning Tom had been—allegedly— shot, by one of his gamekeeper's, during a routine ride through the estate's private grounds. Naturally, Mr Mortimer and I wished to see the horse's corpse. Such a large sum of money couldn't be released without absolute proof of the horse's demise."

"You were refused?" Mr Skinner enquired.

"On the contrary, we were taken directly to the corpse," Mr Ingham replied. "Mr Mortimer was convinced the dead horse was Cunning Tom but I was not."

"May I ask why?" Dr Alexander enquired.

"We weren't permitted to go beyond the stable door, for one, and there was little light to see the corpse by, for two. Mr Duffy's stubborn insistence we make our inspection from a distance gave sufficient cause for my suspicion to be aroused, though. Then, when he refused us more light, my suspicion transformed into conviction," Mr Ingham replied. "When we returned to our office in London, therefore, I made some discreet enquiries among the stable yards and estates close to Castleridge. I met a Groomsman at one such estate—who wishes to remain anonymous for obvious reasons—who told me Cunning Tom was scheduled to arrive there, later this very week, to meet a mare of theirs."

"Was the Groomsman unaware of the horse's demise?" Dr Alexander enquired.

"Far from it. He informed me the arrangement had been made *this very morning* by Mr Duffy on behalf of Lord Castleridge." Mr Ingham shifted in his chair as his expression hardened. "You can imagine my fury, gentlemen, Miss Trent, when I heard this. Without forethought, I travelled to Castleridge and confronted Mr Duffy." He indicated his bruised eye. "This was all I came away with."

"Mr Ingham would like the Bow Street Society to find evidence as to whether Cunning Tom is alive or dead," Miss Trent clarified.

"Did Cunning Tom have any distinguishing, physical features?" Dr Alexander enquired.

"Yes; a patch of white hair, in the centre of his forehead, that very much resembled a Christian cross," Mr Ingham replied.

"That may prove imperative in identifying the animal, though I should be able to tell if a horse has been regularly raced, based on its muscle mass and other factors, provided I'm able to make a thorough examination," Dr Alexander said.

Mr Skinner's expression was thoughtful as he settled back in his chair. "I can tell you if the bullets came from the gamekeeper's gun... but, if the dead horse ain't Cunnin' Tom, Duffy would've got rid of the body by now. You were there this afternoon, correct?"

"Yes," Mr Ingham replied with a firm nod.

"Possibly sold at the Cattle Market on the Caledonian Road, King's Cross," Dr Alexander remarked. "As I understand it, trade is in live animals, but Mr Duffy could've met with an associate there to make an informal arrangement for the corpse."

"Not Sharp's Alley, or the big yard over on Cow-Cross Street, by Farringdon and Smithfield market?" Mr Skinner enquired.

"No. The horse-slaughtering trade declined in that area following the clearance for the Metropolitan Railway. In fact, I believe the cattle market used to be known as the Metropolitan Cattle Market, though I may be mistaken," Dr Alexander explained. "It may be sensible for us to pay the Cattle Market a visit first, to try and locate the corpse before it's sold and made into sausage meat or the like."

"We ought to go to Castleridge, too. If Cunnin' Tom's still there, we should see him with our own two eyes," Mr Skinner interjected.

"Mortimer & Ingham will be generous in its reward should you find evidence of fraudulent activity," Mr Ingham said with half-hearted smile. "Your task shan't be easy to achieve, though. Now Mr Duffy is wise to my suspicions."

"Don't you worry 'bout that, Mr Ingham," Mr Skinner replied as he leaned forward and put his swollen hand down with a soft thud. "I'll deal wit him in my own way."

II

Cruchley's London in 1865: A Handbook for Strangers
stated the cattle market on the "Caledonian Road,
Islington, was opened in 1855, by the late Prince Consort.
It was designed by Mr. Bunning, the City architect; cost
nearly 500,000/... [and had] two taverns on the north side
of the market, public- houses at each corner, twelve
banking-houses, and an electric telegraph office, open only
on market-days, ranged around the clock-tower." By 1896,
the market days were Mondays and Thursdays, while the
clocktower was surrounded by the offices of the market's
officials and clerk. Even without the immense number of
animals present on market day, the sight of empty pens
stretched out across the—supposed—seventy-four acre
area as far as the eye could see was impressive. The
clocktower, too, wouldn't have looked amiss atop a
cathedral; its curved, ornate stonework and pillars added a
touch of majesty to an, oftentimes, foul-smelling arena.

Dr Alexander couldn't help but mark their fortuity
in visiting the establishment on market day. It was late
afternoon when he and Mr Skinner passed through the
imposing, wrought-iron gates and into the trading area
proper. The height of selling had dissipated long before
their arrival, but some last-minute deals were in
negotiation amongst the occupied pens.

The Bow Streeters surveyed the activity from their
vantage point on the crowd's fringe. From what he saw, Dr
Alexander concluded only livestock—live being the
operative word—were being bartered for. He turned
toward Mr Skinner. "It seems we may be too late—"
Something beyond the Irishman caught his attention,
however. Parked by the railings was a flat-bottomed cart
with short sides and wide wheels. Upon it was a bulk
covered by a bloodstained sheet. As he turned, Dr
Alexander witnessed the cart's owner—a tall man in his
early-twenties—lift the sheet's corner to reveal a horse's
head. His associate—a much older man smoking a pipe—

had leaned in close to lift the sheet further and reveal more of the horse.

"Look." Dr Alexander pointed to the pair. "The horse has a white mark on its forehead." Seeing the older man shake his head, release the sheet, and walk away, Dr Alexander seized upon the opportunity to take his place. "Good afternoon," he said once he was within earshot of the younger man. "I noticed you have a dead horse. May I see it?"

"Only if you're serious 'bout buyin' it. Can't be doin' with more gents takin' up my time without good reason." The young man took a deep breath and disturbed the mucus plaguing his nostrils, before compressing the left and expelling a green globule onto the ground with a sharp exhale through the right.

"*Most* serious," Dr Alexander replied. "I'm a veterinary surgeon, and I'm looking for a cadaver to practise upon." He lifted the sheet and pushed it back to rest upon the horse's flank.

Mr Skinner had lingered behind when Dr Alexander approached the cart. The young man was more than a stranger but less than an associate to him. He had little doubt he'd come from the stable hands working beneath Mr Duffy, but he couldn't recall speaking to him. As a result, he'd moved closer to Dr Alexander to within a couple of metres but kept his back to the cart.

"You'll neva find a betta horse than this, then, sir," the young man replied with newfound enthusiasm. "If the price's right, you can take it today."

Dr Alexander ran his hands over the horse's chest and stepped back to gaze upon its entire middle section. Next, he pressed and squeezed the muscles where the shoulders ran into the back. A soft hum left him as his hands paused and then slipped away from the corpse. Stepping aside, he leaned over the horse's head and tilted his own while scrutinising the positioning of a fore leg's origin from a shoulder. When he moved along the cart, toward the horse's rear end, he glanced at Mr Skinner but the Irishman's back remained to him. "May I know where the horse came from?" Dr Alexander enquired from the younger man while he lifted the sheet and dipped his head to peer between the animal's hind legs. Lifting its tail, he slipped his hand between the upper thighs to press and squeeze the muscles.

"A respeckible gent, sir," the young man replied.

Dr Alexander dropped the tail and, returning to the horse's front, leaned over it to scrutinise the white cross on its forehead. Even without touching it he could distinguish the dried flakes of white paint in the animal's otherwise golden chestnut coloured fur. "I'll buy him," Dr Alexander announced. Taking a large bank note from his purse, he passed it across to the wide-eyed, young man. "I trust this will suffice?"

"Y-Yes, sir. Thank you."

"Excellent. Could you stay with the cart until I make the necessary arrangements for the corpse to be taken to my practise?" Dr Alexander enquired. Once the young man had given his assent, Dr Alexander smiled and walked with Mr Skinner to the gates. As he did so, he explained in a soft voice. "Aside from the obvious use of paint to create the mark on the animal's forehead, the lack of substance in the muscles of its hind quarters and shoulders—not to mention its overtly broad chest—would render it useless as a race horse. I have serious doubt it could've been a capable cart horse, even."

"Were there any bullet wounds?"

"None." Dr Alexander turned out of the cattle market. "You were rather hesitant, I noticed."

"I recognised the lad as one of Duffy's men. I couldn't be sure he hadn't known me, so I kept my distance. We don't want 'im tellin' Duffy I bought the horse he showed Ingham & Mortimer as Cunnin' Tom." Mr Skinner stopped at the roadside to glance back through the gates. "We should visit Castleridge once we've got this done, try and find the real Cunnin' Tom before 'e's moved. If we can do that, and show this dead one to

Ingham & Mortimer, both Duffy and Lord Castleridge'll have to drop the claim."

"I agree." Dr Alexander crossed the street with his associate as he added, "Let us get to it, then."

III

Six thirty. Dr Alexander snapped his pocket watch shut and slipped it beneath the doors of Mr Snyder's cab. Despite the—relatively—early hour, a bitterly cold darkness had descended upon them. They'd left the commotion of London over two hours' previous for the bleak sparseness of ditch-lined countryside tracks. Vast abysses, hiding familiar sights of fields and trees, lay beyond what could be distinguished in the weak glow of the cab's Davey lamp. Dr Alexander tucked his hands beneath the blanket over his knees and shuffled it up his arms. Meanwhile, Mr Skinner sat with his swollen hand rested upon the doors' top edge and a lit cigarette in his other. He'd declined a blanket from Mr Snyder—much to Dr Alexander's surprise—and, presently, showed no signs of feeling the cold.

"Not much farther, now," Mr Skinner remarked and discarded his cigarette into the darkness.

"You know Castleridge well, then?"

Mr Skinner leaned back into the darkness of the cab. "My master, Captain Mirrell, is friends wit Lord Castleridge. I've gone there, with Lady Mirrell, when there's been a hunt on."

Dr Alexander heard rummaging coming from Mr Skinner's side but couldn't see what he was doing. A soft click, followed by the whirl of a gun's barrel, and a loud snap, answered his curiousity, however. "You've come armed?"

"Always, Doctor." More rummaging. "Especially when speakin' to Mr Duffy. As you've seen, violence's the only language he understands."

"Yes, but surely he wouldn't attack us—"

"They call 'im Mr Fear, and not just because his middle name's Feardorcha. When we meet 'im, let me do the talkin'."

Dr Alexander swallowed but gave an indistinguishable nod within the darkness. "In that case, my life's in your hands… Mr Skinner."

They felt the cab turn and heard the crack of Mr Snyder's whip. The track opened out ahead of them and, within moments, a set of iron, double gates came into view. As the cab slowed to a stop, a man wearing a flat cap emerged from a small, stone-built, thatched-roofed lodge stood to the gates' right.

"Evenin'!" The man called as he trudged through the mud and stood by the cab, a storm lamp in his hand. Looking to Mr Snyder, he enquired, "Who might you be, then? His Lordship's not expectin' any visitors this eve."

"We're 'ere to see Mr Duffy in the stables," Mr Skinner interjected, leaning across Dr Alexander and the cab's doors. "You remember me, don't you, Reg? Mr Callahan Skinner. I come by wit Captain and Lady Mirrell last month."

The man lifted the storm lamp to illuminate the cab's interior. While Dr Alexander shielded his eyes, Mr Skinner didn't move. Reg looked between them and nodded. "I remember you, Mr Skinner. Mr Duffy's never said you'd be coming by tonight. I'll have to get the lad to fetch 'im."

"Please, do that," Mr Skinner replied. "We'll wait 'ere."

Reg withdrew his lamp, thereby plunging the cab into darkness, and trudged back to his lodge. A few moments later, a lanky-looking lad emerged and ran into the darkness. He pulled on a cloth cap as he went, but paid no attention to the cab or its occupants.

"He's watching us," Dr Alexander remarked.

Mr Skinner looked to the lodge and saw Reg's face in a ground floor window. "Watchin' the gate's 'is job, Doctor." Mr Skinner unfastened the cab's doors and climbed out.

Following his lead, Dr Alexander then glanced up at Mr Snyder as he handed him the cab's Davey lamp. "Thank you…" Dr Alexander grimaced.

"I'll be righ' 'ere, should you need me," Mr

Snyder told him.

"The less of us that speak to Duffy, the better," Mr Skinner remarked. He put his back to the lodge and rested his hand upon the butt of a Webley Mark I revolver holstered beneath his coat. Satisfied it was within reach, he dropped his coat closed and retrieved a loose cigarette from his pocket. "Want one?"

"No… thank you," Dr Alexander replied and watched as his fellow Bow Streeter lit the cigarette one handed using a match. However, Dr Alexander's gaze soon wandered to Mr Skinner's right hand. It rested on his stomach but retained an obvious rigidity in its fingers. "Forgive me, Mr Skinner, but have you injured your hand?"

"No." Mr Skinner walked toward the—still locked—iron gates as a cold wind blew through them. The trees which lined the snake-like driveway beyond also danced and swayed with a near-deafening rustle. Every now and then, yellow dots of light broke through the otherwise dense barrier of foliage, betraying the location of the Castleridge home. Somewhere in the distance the sudden screech of a fox sounded and caused Dr Alexander to turn sharply.

Mr Skinner smirked. "I thought you were a vet, Doctor?"

"I am, but I'm unaccustomed to the uncanniness of an isolated country estate in the middle of the night."

"Still early." Mr Skinner shrugged a shoulder. "Her Ladyship won't have had dinner, yet." He listened to Dr Alexander's approach to join him at the gates.

"How did you come to be her bodyguard, if I may enquire?"

"Why do you want to know?" Mr Skinner looked sideways at him and exhaled a cloud of smoke that dissipated between them.

"You're entrusting your life as much as I am. It makes sense for us to one we're putting so much faith in, doesn't it?"

"It does." Mr Skinner turned back toward the gates. "Seems like all the talk's been 'bout me, though." He dropped the cigarette and crushed it beneath his boot's heel.

Dr Alexander took a moment's consideration. "Yes, I suppose it has…" He smiled. "To balance the scale, you may ask me anything."

"Why'd you join the Society?"

"The same reason as most; I want to help others in whatever way I can. I graduated from the Royal Veterinary College after taking their three-year course. I now run a private practise of my own in addition to my charity work at the Poor-People's Outpatient Clinic. I tend to sick animals regardless of their owners' social status."

"That's very noble of you, Doctor," Mr Skinner remarked, followed by silence while he, too, took a moment for consideration. "Captain Mirrell was my commanding officer on board ship when I was honourably discharged from the Navy. He wanted protection for his wife—someone he could trust while he was away at sea. He asked me, and I agreed. That were eight years ago."

"I see." Dr Alexander smiled. "And your hand…?"

The sounds of trudging feet then reached them, however, drawing their attention back to the matter at hand.

A ball of light soon emerged from the darkness, growing in size with every passing moment. When it had come closer still, the form of a man in his early forties became visible within its range. He wore a shin length dark brown coat with broad cuffs and lapels. The light's source was revealed as a storm lamp as the man stopped a few metres away from the gates and held it at arm's length to illuminate the Bow Streeter's faces. At the same time, his own features became more defined; dark-grey stubble covered his chin and upper lip beneath an enlarged nose. His black hair was thick on top but sparse in his sideburns.

The emaciated, young lad—who'd hurried along a few paces behind—stood at his elbow.

"Callahan, what in the world are ye doin' disturbin' me at this hour? Don't ye know it's puttin' away time," the elder man enquired with a soft, Irish twang and the faint scent of whiskey on his breath. "Lad says ye asked fer me in particular."

"Beggin' your pardon, Mr Duffy." Mr Skinner stepped forward. "But me and my friend, 'ere, wanna talk to you about Cunnin' Tom."

Mr Duffy's expression hardened but his pale, blue eyes remained transfixed by his fellow Irishman. "Best go inside, lad." The boy obeyed without hesitation, but Duffy didn't continue until he'd heard the lodge door close. "Cunnin' Tom's dead."

"So we've 'eard," Mr Skinner replied.

"Then why's it your business?"

"Mr Ingham don't believe 'e is."

Mr Duffy's lips curled into a sneer. "Who'd ye say your friend were…?"

"Doctor Rupert Alexander. 'E's a vet, come to see Cunnin' Tom."

Mr Duffy closed the distance between them. "Ingham already saw 'is body. It don't take a vet to know the beast's dead."

Mr Skinner returned the favour of encroaching upon his fellow Irishman's personal space. For all the gates were between them, the steam created by their breaths dissipated into the others' faces. Mr Skinner's voice was cool when he said, "We're know you're lyin', Mr Duffy, for we've seen the dead horse you told Mr Ingham and Mr Mortimer were Cunnin' Tom this mornin'. Not just this, but Dr Alexander 'ere bought the body for a princely sum from your Mr O'Donnell at the cattle market and is willin' to swear—under oath—the horse 'e bought couldn't have run a mile."

Mr Duffy's eyes narrowed as they swept across to Dr Alexander and back to Mr Skinner. "If Mr O'Donnell were sellin' a dead, lame horse at the market, it's got nowt to do with me—or Lord Castleridge. Now, be on your way!" Mr Duffy turned from the gates and Mr Skinner caught a glimpse of a shotgun hidden beneath Duffy's coat. "B'fore I set the dogs on ye!"

"Dogs…?" Dr Alexander enquired in a quiet voice.

"Ge' in the cab." Mr Skinner walked backward from the gates, keeping his gaze on Duffy's fading form until the last moment, and climbed into the cab. Once Dr Alexander joined him, he knocked on the roof and slammed the doors shut. As he felt the vehicle lurch forward and start to turn, he retrieved his revolver to rest upon his knee. Dr Alexander, meanwhile, was engrossed in silent contemplation of the man, and reception, they'd just encountered.

The cab was permitted to travel a couple of miles down the country track before Mr Skinner knocked on the roof. "Stop 'ere!" He called and reopened the doors.

"What are you doing?" Dr Alexander enquired as his fellow Bow Streeter climbed out onto the muddy trackside. When he received no answer, he slid across the seat to follow. In the dim light of the Davey lamp, he saw the glint of the revolver's barrel as Mr Skinner readied it. "You *can't* be *seriously* considering such a course of action?"

"The gun's just for protection." Mr Skinner slipped the revolver back into its holster. "Any other time, I'd tell you to stay 'ere, Doctor. But this needs the both of us."

"I'm well aware of that." Dr Alexander placed a hand upon Mr Skinner's shoulder to stay him. "But I never agreed to violence. Should it come to that, I'll have no part in it. Do you understand?"

"I don't want Duffy findin' us in there any more than you do, Doctor." Mr Skinner looked up at Mr Snyder, who sat on his seat set high on the cab's rear. "Drive on a couple of miles and then wait for ten minutes before comin' back. We'll be waitin' for you 'ere when you do."

"Okay," Mr Snyder replied with a touch of his broad-brimmed hat.

"We can climb over the wall near 'ere," Mr Skinner said, addressing Dr Alexander. "We'll have to keep to the wall, and in the shadow of the trees, but we can get to the stable yard within the half hour. All we need's a look at Cunnin' Tom. Then we can get back to Bow Street and Miss Trent." Mr Skinner stepped past him and strode along the track's edge, using the hedge row's faint outline to guide him. When he heard Dr Alexander following, he continued, "Did you see the look Duffy gave us when we said we'd bought the dead horse? Cunnin' Tom's still in there."

Dr Alexander was breathing heavier by the time he fell into step beside him. Despite their proximity, Mr Skinner's silhouette was faint against the pitch blackness. Every now and then, he felt Mr Skinner's coat brush against his knuckles. This, in turn, obliged him to increase the space between them. He took some comfort in being the closest to the track's centre, however. "Wouldn't it be wiser to wait until the morning and try, again, to see the horse? You said yourself that Mr Duffy's dangerous. If he catches us, prowling around the stable yard, he'll do more than simply call a constable, shan't he?"

"It'll be too late by mornin'. Duffy's probably movin' Cunnin' Tom to a different hidin' place already. We'll have no chance of findin' him if we wait. It's gotta be tonight." Mr Skinner halted. "Are you wit me or not?"

Dr Alexander halted, too, and a gust of wind filled the subsequent silence.

"Very well…" he replied after some contemplation. "I'm with you." A hand then gripped and tugged upon his arm, followed by the rapid sounds of boots squishing through mud. As he followed, he mumbled, "May God protect us…"

IV

A soft grunt sounded from Mr Skinner as he pulled himself up and onto the wall. It was over six feet tall with gigantic bramble bushes growing against its brickwork. Hooking his right hand onto the wall's inside edge, he dropped his left to provide Dr Alexander enough lift to hoist himself off the ground. The tips of Dr Alexander's feet scrambled against the brickwork at the same time and, in mere moments, he was beside the Irishman. A heartbeat later and Mr Skinner lowered himself down to the ground. Glancing down to gauge the wall's depth, therefore, Dr Alexander swung his legs around and turned to follow his fellow Bow Streeter.

"The house's over there, where them lights are," Mr Skinner said softly, through the darkness once the two were beneath the canopy of a willow tree. "We're goin' to the right. Keep close to me."

"Of course," Dr Alexander whispered. Catching the faint outline of Mr Skinner's silhouette when he crouched down, Dr Alexander did the same and scurried across the pristine—if damp—lawn. The dense foliage of the trees, tall hedges, and overstuffed flower beds provided enough cover for them to traverse the gardens without being seen. Wherein the daytime they would've had the gardeners to avoid, they were alone in the night. Picking up the faint—yet distinctive—scent of animal manure on the air as they left the garden proper, Dr Alexander straightened and hurried to stand by Mr Skinner against the trunk of an old oak tree. Up ahead, a collection of ancient trees separated to reveal a long, wooden gate. The wind carried the sound of men's muffled voices from beyond the gate to where they were concealed.

"Stable's over there," Mr Skinner said, and for a second time, Dr Alexander heard the click of the revolver being prepared.

"Look," Dr Alexander replied and pointed to a group of men who'd come through the gate. At their head was Mr Duffy and, amongst them, a fine-looking horse led on by a stable hand. Lamps, which the men carried, illuminated their group enough for Dr Alexander to distinguish the horse's round and well-proportioned chest; an excellent sign its respiratory system could help sustain a fast pace for extended periods of time. It also appeared to be above the average height of fifteen hands two inches— or sixty-two inches, or five feet two inches—which would be expected from a racehorse. Finally, its thigh muscles were well-developed and of sufficient length to provide firm propulsion for a horse expected to run competitively. However, the most convincing piece of evidence as to the animal's identity came in the form of a white cross in the centre of its forehead. He gripped Mr Skinner's arm.

"I see it."

Dr Alexander heard Mr Skinner's hurried feet push through the long grass.

"Let's follow 'em."

The group of men followed the path through the trees, their lamps like fireflies, enabling Mr Skinner and Dr Alexander to follow at a considerable distance. When the balls of light eventually broke rank to spread out amongst the trees, Dr Alexander dropped into a crouch and hid behind bush. He suspected the group had reached a clearing—based upon the formation they'd taken—but the almost impenetrable darkness made it difficult to be certain.

"O'Donnell, ye'll come back fer 'im at first light," Duffy's voice ordered after a few minutes had passed, followed by a reply muffled by the rustling of leaves overheard.

Seeing the fireflies regroup and retrace their steps along the path, Dr Alexander ducked lower behind the bush until their light faded in the distance. "Mr Skinner…?" he hissed.

"Righ' behind you, Doctor." Mr Skinner's hand tugged upon Dr Alexander's shoulder as he rose and, once again, pushed through the long grass toward the now vacant area.

Dr Alexander's attempt to follow was momentarily thwarted by the cuff of his jacket becoming caught on the bush's thorns. With a sharp tug, and tearing of fabric, he managed to free himself, though. Scuffing his shoulders against various trees as he went, he was relieved to feel the damp, soft grass shift into a firmer layer of mud and stones beneath his feet when he entered the clearing. Against the darkness, he saw the near-invisible line of the sloped roof and square walls of a brick-built building. He was only certain of its material due to his toes striking it as he approached and his hand—that he'd thrown out to steady himself with—feeling the rough texture of the bricks and mortar. The sound of waves lapping against the shore reached him from behind the structure—a lake, perhaps? Whatever it was, it paled in significance compared to the distinct clopping of horses' hooves against stone which he heard from *within* the building.

Putting his other hand with the first, he used the wall to guide him around the structure while sidestepping through the mud. A sudden collision with something soft, and the quiet grunt that accompanied it, compelled him to mutter, "My apologies, Mr Skinner."

"Don't worry; I can't see a t'ing either. Do you hear what I do?"

"Yes, but we'll need to see inside to be certain. Have you found a door, or a window, perhaps?"

"I think there's a window above us. If you stand on my knee, you should be able to look through it."

"Very well…" Dr Alexander turned but kept one hand on the wall while his other felt around in the darkness. When it found Mr Skinner's knee, Dr Alexander lifted his opposite foot to rest upon it. Next, he shifted his hand to Mr Skinner's shoulder and hoisted himself up while reaching out for the window ledge. Fortunately, he found it on the first attempt and turned to peer over its edge and into the building.

A single lamp hung from the high ceiling, illuminating the horse beneath. The animal had been given straw and feed in his makeshift stable. Yet, despite this, its distress at being in an unfamiliar, confined space was obvious. Dr Alexander frowned. His first instinct was to find the door and lead the horse away—if only for the sake of its wellbeing. He knew both he and Mr Skinner could be prosecuted for horse rustling, though. He therefore lowered himself back to the ground—albeit with great reluctance—and whispered, "I think it's time we enlisted the police's assistance. The poor beast is in great distress and I can't, in good conscience, leave it without knowing it will be helped."

"Horse belongs to Lord Castleridge," Mr Skinner reminded him. "We can't jus' walk it out of 'ere wit it, even wit the police's help. You also heard what Duffy told Mr O'Donnell; 'e wants 'im to come back for the horse at dawn. That means they'll take it either to their stables or to someone else's nearby."

"Then we'll return before dawn—*with* a police officer of rank and Messrs Ingham and Mortimer—to confront both Lord Castleridge and Mr Duffy over this entire business."

"And the dead horse?"

"When we return to Bow Street, I'll arrange with Miss Trent for the police to bring it on a cart. Like you said; we must give Lord Castleridge and Mr Duffy no option but to abandon their insurance claim. Showing them we have the corpse, and proving we know where the *real* Cunning Tom is, should do that."

Mr Skinner took a moment of consideration. "You're right," he said, finally. "And, as long as we're not caught goin' out of 'ere, there's no reason for Mr Duffy to move Cunnin' Tom again tonight."

"Exactly," Dr Alexander replied in triumph.

V

"This is highly irregular, not to mention inconvenient," Mr Mortimer remarked. He was older than his business partner by at least a decade. Though his hair was thick, it had turned grey, while his whiskers retained their coal-black colour. A shiver ran through him, and he tightened the blanket around his shoulders. Beside him sat Mr Ingham, Mr Skinner, and Dr Alexander. They sat within Mr Snyder's cab that, in turn, was parked outside the grand house of the Castleridge estate. Behind the Bow Street Society vehicle was a large, horse drawn van driven by a uniformed constable under Inspector John Conway's watch.

A veteran Metropolitan Police officer, and Head of the Criminal Investigation Department's Mob Squad, Conway was middle-aged with fair, weathered features. His neat, dark-red hair was covered by a black trilby hat, while his beard and moustache were trimmed. Beneath the knee-length, black overcoat he wore was a dark-grey suit with a midnight-blue waistcoat and matching tie framed by a starched, white Eton collar.

"And to involve the *police*…" Mr Mortimer continued, "…If *that* had been our desire, we would have sought their assistance from the beginning. *Discretion* was our intention, Mr Skinner. The Bow Street Society has forfeited that luxury and for what? An absurd hope that Lord Castleridge shall crumple to his knees and beg for our mercy the moment he's informed we have his dead horse," Mr Mortimer grunted in distaste. "If scandal should be brought to our firm as a result of this encounter, I shall hold the Bow Street Society *personally* responsible—financially or otherwise."

"With all due respect, Mr Mortimer, we are doing what we were commissioned to do," Dr Alexander pointed out.

The house's immense double doors opened and two silhouettes emerged from an electricity fuelled golden glow. Mr Duffy's fierce countenance turned into the light, which bounced off the shotgun in his hands. His associate was taller and younger—in his late thirties at the most—with an unblemished face framed by iridescent brown hair. His pale-green eyes were sharp as they took in the scene before him. Mr Skinner, Mr Ingham, and Dr Alexander had alighted. Mr Mortimer now followed—albeit with great reluctance—while Inspector Conway moved to join the Bow Streeters.

"*Mr* Ingham, you'd better have a good reason for rousing me from my slumber and exposing me to this harsh, winter morn," the unknown gentleman remarked. "*What* was so important it not only couldn't wait until after daybreak, but couldn't be dealt with by anyone else but *me*? You know Mr Duffy is my representative where the stables are concerned."

"I do, your lordship," Mr Ingham replied and stepped forward. "May I first introduce my business partner, Mr Mortimer, and the representatives of the Bow Street Society, Mr Skinner and Dr Alexander?"

"You may, but it doesn't answer my questions, sir," Lord Castleridge retorted and turned toward Conway. "And this man…?"

The grizzled policeman approached with his warrant card held aloft. "Inspector John Conway from Scotland Yard, sir. I'm here at the Bow Street Society's invitation because there's been an accusation of insurance fraud. Something about a lame horse being put out as your dead, prize racehorse."

"I presume you have proof of your abhorrent allegations?" Lord Castleridge enquired. "Otherwise Commissioner Bradford shall hear of this."

"We have the dead horse—that Mr O'Donnell, one of your stable hands—sold to us at the Cattle Market," Mr Skinner replied. "The same horse your man, Mr Duffy, told Mr Mortimer and Mr Ingham were your prize racehorse, Cunnin' Tom—who's in a hut near the lake on your grounds."

"*Preposterous!*" Lord Castleridge exclaimed.

"Then you shan't object to Inspector Conway and his constable searching it, shall you?" Dr Alexander interjected.

"I do, and I shall," Lord Castleridge snapped and walked down the steps with Mr Duffy at his back. "This is a breach of my privacy and rights as an English nobleman, Inspector. While I have doubts you understand the significance of my status, you will soon come to know its degree of influence when I have you stripped of your rank and sent to the workhouse. If you do not wish to see this come to pass, I suggest you remove these men from my land at once."

"Got somethin' to hide?" Mr Skinner enquired.

"Pay no heed to this man, Your Lordship," Mr Mortimer interjected as he gave a brief dip of his head. "We apologise, profusely, for this intrusion on your property and privacy—"

"I think the matter can be resolved easily enough," Dr Alexander said. "We have strong reason to believe Cunning Tom—the horse you are attempting to claim a large sum of money from your insurance policy on—is alive and concealed in the hut. I'm a veterinarian surgeon by profession, Your Lordship. As a result, my concern is the horse's welfare. Should you refuse to allow the Inspector to search the hut, then I will be obliged to press him in returning with a mob of constables. They'll trample your lawn, arouse the attention of your neighbours, and cause you more scandal than his visit now would cause. Alternatively, you may drop your insurance claim and Inspector Conway shall leave without intruding upon your privacy further. Either way, I demand you permit me to examine your racehorse—alone—for signs of distress which may impede its capacity as a stud horse."

"I don't have to tolerate this veiled attempt at blackmail, Doctor," Lord Castleridge retorted.

"Perhaps you would like to see the dead horse, then?" Dr Alexander enquired and withdrew from the light to approach the van. Lord Castleridge and Mr Duffy exchanged glances but the former soon followed the veterinarian surgeon nonetheless. The others stepped aside but then joined the trio at the van's rear when Dr Alexander opened its doors. Impeded by the darkness, Dr Alexander retrieved a Davey lamp from the constable to hold it aloft and thereby illuminate the van's interior. When its weak glow fell upon a horse's corpse, Lord Castleridge and Mr Duffy leaned forward for a closer look.

"Looks like Cunnin' Tom to me," Mr Duffy remarked.

"At first glance, yes. I doubt his lordship's prize racehorse has white paint smeared across its forehead, though... do you?" Dr Alexander said and brushed out the dried flakes from the horse's hair with his hand.

Lord Castleridge glared at his head groomsman. "Mr Duffy, this is beyond abhorrent. You attempt to deceive these men for your own, personal gain at the expense of my honour and reputation—?"

"The insurance claim was written in your hand, Your Lordship," Mr Skinner interjected as he held up a letter given to him by Messrs Ingham and Mortimer during their journey there. "And on your notepaper."

Lord Castleridge reeled back from the van to stare at the insurance brokers. "A forgery... one written by an expert hand but-but a forgery all the same. Mr Duffy... have you any explanation for this...?"

"I can think of a couple, Milord," Mr Duffy replied as he set his shotgun upon the van's floor. "None of them have me goin' to Newgate for ye." He looked to Mr Skinner. "That letter's no forgery." He placed a hand on the dead horse's neck. "And yer right; this ain't Cunnin' Tom." Retrieving his shotgun, he slammed the doors shut and walked past Dr Alexander, toward the wooded area of the garden. "If ye wanna see the real Cunnin' Tom, ye'd best come wit me, Doctor."

"I'd like to come, if you don't mind," Mr Skinner said.

Mr Duffy stopped and looked back over his shoulder. "Suit yeself."

"Wait a minute," Lord Castleridge said. "Whatever you may think, Mr Duffy, you are still employed by *me*. You shan't go anywhere without my approval." He advanced upon Messrs Ingham and Mortimer, but only Mortimer recoiled. "As for you both, if—and I'm only saying if—the dead horse in this van is *not* Cunning Tom, and I'm willing to admit as much and withdraw my insurance claim, do I have your word as gentlemen that no further action—legal or otherwise— shall be taken against me?"

"You do," Mr Ingham replied.

Lord Castleridge gave a small nod. "Good." He glanced at Mr Duffy. "Take Dr Alexander and his associate to examine Cunning Tom. Messrs Ingham and Mortimer, I'll write you first thing in the morning to withdraw my claim against Cunning Tom's insurance policy. In return, there will be no further developments in this matter. Agreed?" He extended his hand to them.

"Agreed," Mr Ingham replied without hesitation and gave the lord's hand a firm shake. Only when Mr Mortimer did the same did Dr Alexander, Mr Skinner, and Mr Duffy leave the group to venture through the trees and to the hut by the lake.

Meanwhile, Inspector Conway returned to his constable's side atop the van with the passing thought of Miss Trent receiving a cheque for a large sum of money in tomorrow's afternoon post. A smile danced upon his lips at the imagined look upon her face when she opened the envelope. *Yet another successful case for the Bow Street Society...* He mused and indicated the driveway. "Let's get this horse to the knackers' yard."

The Case of the Peculiar Portrait

I

"Thank you for agreeing to this consultation, Miss Trent, despite my impertinence," Mrs Clementine Barker said as she watched the cream billow into her tea. Her quiet voice was further muffled by her lace veil and frequent glances to the parlour door.

Compared to Miss Trent's slender five foot seven inches form, the diminutive nature of Mrs Barker's build was blatant. A cotton bustle dress, topped with a satin, rose-print overlay and trimmed with lace concealed a tight corset. It, the veil, and gloves covered her skin with black, thus making the assessment of her age, appearance, and social class difficult. Yet, the Bow Street Society clerk attempted to determine them nonetheless. Based upon the occasional glimpse of vivid, blond ringlets through the veil and the strength of Mrs Barker's vocal chords, Miss Trent placed her age somewhere between twenty-five and thirty-five.

By contrast, Miss Trent's attire comprised of a ruffle-necked, satin blouse and a set of high-waist bustle skirt. The former was plain with a cameo pinned to the collar's centre, underneath the ruffled edge. Her skirt, meanwhile, was a combination of plain and patterned panels. The blouse, plain panels, and embroidered, rose pattern were dark purple in colour, with the last set against a cream background. Her shoulder-length, chestnut-brown hair was styled into tight, corkscrew curls, some of which framed her fair, unblemished face. Though also in her late-twenties, Miss Trent's voice held far more life than her would-be client's. Furthermore, her dark-brown eyes never strayed.

"Not impertinence, Mrs Barker, but practicality. Bow Street Society clients rarely require formal introductions because, in most instances, they're a waste of valuable time. You wanted to speak to me urgently, and I was in a position to grant your request. May I ask why you had your maid wait in the hallway, though, when she accompanied you here?"

"Respectable women mustn't travel alone, but this matter isn't for a servant's ears."

"Very well." Miss Trent set down her cup and saucer to retrieve her notebook and pencil laid beside the tray. "How may we help you this morning?"

Mrs Barker sat upon a high, triple balloon-shaped back tête-à-tête sofa that faced a large fireplace. The Bow Street Society clerk had taken the matching, overstuffed armchair to the sofa's left, facing the parlour door. Each piece was upholstered in a navy-blue fabric adorned with light-blue, embroidered leaves to mirror the rug laid out beneath a low table between the sofa and chair. Even the walls had a light-blue, leaf design to their bronze gilt wallpaper. Members' donations, recently added to the room, included a music box amongst the Dickens' tomes upon the bookshelf and a taxidermy herring housed in a glass case on a table behind the door.

"It's difficult to explain." Mrs Barker bowed her head. "I've had a terrible time of it, trying to decide if I should seek the Society's help at all. My husband's reassurances have brought me some comfort, but then the happenings recur, and I am once again plunged into the depths of despair." Mrs Barker partially lifted her veil to sip her tea. "Please, forgive me." She dropped the veil back into place. "I'm making little sense but, even now, I'm conflicted. I've heard much of your group—

particularly the fine work it has done for others—and don't wish to put either its time or resources to waste."

"Part of my role as the Society's clerk is to decide whether we accept a commission. I therefore need to hear the facts from each potential client we have. Rest assured, even if your case is declined, you wouldn't have wasted anything." Miss Trent attempted to meet Mrs Barker's gaze through the veil. "Whatever your problem is, it's clearly caused you great distress."

Mrs Barker hesitated long enough for Miss Trent to suspect she was about to flee. Her lack of movement and visible expression compelled Miss Trent to hold her tongue, however. After several moments passed, Mrs Barker rewarded Miss Trent's patience by folding back her veil. Her face was rounded and doll-like in its features. The robust, blue eyes and faint crow's feet supported Miss Trent's earlier conclusion as to Mrs Barker's age.

"Thank you for your patience. I'm prone to hysteria… the events of these past few weeks have only served to strengthen it." Mrs Barker balanced her teacup and saucer in her lap. "Six months ago, my first husband—Jeffrey Downton—drowned in the River Thames while he, myself, and our mutual friend, Mr Creighton Barker, were swimming."

Miss Trent lofted a brow but begun her notes.

"I can surmise your thoughts, and they would be correct. Mr Barker and I married three months ago. His proposal was born from a desire to look after his late friend's one, true love. He saw it as a way of honouring Jeffrey's memory. Creighton has been most generous with his patience and understanding since the happenings began." Her hands trembled against the teacup, and she took a shallow breath. "I'm being haunted—I'm convinced of it. The soul of my dear, departed Jeffrey isn't at rest—and never could be—for, you see, his death was by my hand."

Miss Trent's pencil paused. "Please, elaborate further, Mrs Barker…" Her tone was grave and, while awaiting the answer, she reflected upon the potential repercussions of not having more witnesses to hear the confession.

"Jeffrey didn't wish to go swimming in the Thames—he said it was wretchedly filthy—but *I* insisted. I was told its waters would rid me of a tiresome cough. I should have *listened* to him…" She gave a soft sob. "His body was found several miles downriver, washed up amongst timber and other unspeakable pollution."

"Why do you believe he's haunting you?"

"Jeffrey was photographed a year before he died. It's the only likeness I have of him—that both I *and* Creighton have of him. We'd therefore hung it in our parlour at home. Yet, a month ago, while I was sewing by the fire, I happened to look up at the portrait…" Her face turned the same shade of white as her teacup. "…Jeffrey had *vanished*!"

"The portrait was missing?"

"No, the frame and photograph were in place, but Jeffrey *wasn't*. Where he had been standing was naught but the curtain and scenery. I fled from the room at once and sought out Creighton. We returned together and…" Her hand shook as she placed the teacup upon the tray. "…Footprints, Miss Trent… *wet* footprints…" Mrs Barker pressed her handkerchief against her nose, and tears ran down her cheeks. "They began at the fireplace and came toward us…"

"What was your husband's reaction?" Miss Trent

continued her notes with more fervour.

"He didn't see either the footprints or the empty photograph. He *insisted* the rug was dry, and Jeffrey was still there. He even led me back to the portrait to prove it to me but, alas, my senses continued to be deceptive until the next morning when I saw the truth of it."

"Jeffrey had returned?"

"Indeed." Mrs Barker gave a gentle sniff and dabbed at the underside of her nose. "Creighton forgave my foolishness. Yet, I cannot forget those footprints…" Mrs Barker lowered her handkerchief. "Creighton knows of my strain… It's why we are here in London. He's arranged for us to attend the Savoy Theatre tonight with some friends of ours. We're staying at the hotel on Henrietta Street."

"And the portrait…?" Miss Trent looked up.

Mrs Barker grimaced. "It hangs upon the wall in our suite. I didn't want to bring it, but Creighton reminded me of its importance to us both. He wanted Jeffrey to share our enjoyment while in London, if only in spirit." Mrs Barker shuddered. "I can't bear to look upon it, Miss Trent. I am too afraid of what mightn't be there."

Miss Trent closed her notebook. "Our members will have to see it, though, Mrs Barker, if they're to have any hope of discovering the cause of these happenings."

"Yes… of course…" Mrs Barker replaced her veil. "But Creighton is unaware of this visit. I didn't want to worry him further, you see. He would have tried to reassure me, but even he can do little to ease my distress now. I must know if I'm mad or if…" Another sob sounded from beyond the lace as Mrs Barker stood like a jack-in-the-box. She at once turned toward the door but paused to add, "Creighton is having luncheon with a business associate at midday today. Miss Doris Cooper, my maid, will also be out visiting her family in Stepney." Mrs Barker put her hand upon the parlour door's knob, "We are in room thirteen." She then left the room to collect her servant while Miss Trent rose to unbolt the front door.

II

Located in Westminster, Henrietta Street was but a short cab ride from Bow Street. It was therefore close enough to the Royal Opera House on that thoroughfare and the Savoy Theatre—that adjoined the prestigious Savoy Hotel—to be convenient. Yet, still far enough to avoid the inevitable noise caused by the crowds of stage connoisseurs as they journeyed home.

The hotel where the Barkers stayed wasn't as luxurious as the Savoy, but it boasted a reputation of respectability among the middle classes nonetheless. Its front elevation comprised of stone, arched doorways bookending four, tall, square windows. Iron railings lined the hotel's perimeter and followed the doors' shallow flights of stone steps. The hotel's lounge, filled with overstuffed armchairs and faux antiques could be seen beyond the windows. An immense, decorative, oak fireplace housed an equally impressive hearth where a strong fire burned. Its light illuminated the room with an orange glow, accentuated by nearby low-burning kerosene lamps and brass, candlelit chandeliers. Veteran businessmen, dour-faced widows, and young ladies— chaperoned by paid companions—made up the hotel's middle-class clientele.

Though the air was mild, a gloom had fallen upon Henrietta Street due to dense cloud cover. Mr Virgil Verity therefore turned his gaze skyward as he alighted from the Bow Street Society's cab. He was pleased to see light-grey clouds rather than dark; there was sufficient time to get inside before the rain, at least.

A wholesome, off-white beard, moustache, and wrinkle-riddled, grey complexion denoted his sixty years.

Yet, despite his advanced age, he had a full head of thick, silver hair. His chosen attire was a dark-green and brown tweed suit with a black waistcoat beneath. Both were hidden under a thick, black, woollen overcoat that hung to his ankles, a knitted, dark-green scarf, and broad-brimmed, brown hat. Hearing his companion alight from the cab also, he shuffled around to offer her his arm.

Miss Georgina Dexter placed her slender hand in the crook of his elbow as she graced him with a warm smile. Like Mr Verity, she wore a heavy, winter coat—hers being midnight-blue in colour. Beneath, she wore a modest, pale-blue dress with a high, ruffled neck and straight-lined skirts. A midnight-blue bonnet, lined with black lace, sat atop her head and provided the perfect backdrop to her pinned, auburn hair. Like Mr Verity, Miss Dexter was fair skinned, but hers was unblemished by the passage of time. Her green eyes were also as keen as his brown. Due to her petite build—and Mr Verity's stoop as he walked—it would appear to the casual observer that they were the same height. In reality, Mr Verity was taller than Miss Dexter by two feet, she being five foot exactly. The obvious difference in age—there were forty-two years between them—meant they could be mistaken for grandfather and granddaughter, too. Nevertheless, they entered the hotel together and sought out room thirteen on the second floor.

"Mrs Clementine Barker?" Mr Verity enquired from the young lady who opened its door. For a moment, his strong, Tyneside accent had cast the shadow of confusion upon her features.

When she'd fathomed her own name from his statement, she gave a polite smile. "Oh, yes... I'm she, and you are...?"

"Are you alone?" Mr Verity enquired.

"I am," Mrs Barker replied.

"Then I'm Mr Virgil Verity, a retired schoolteacher and spiritualist, and this is Miss Georgina Dexter, a freelance artist with a knack for photography. We're also members of the Bow Street Society. Miss Trent sent us."

Mrs Barker stepped aside at once. "Please, come in." She closed the door behind them. "May I presume Miss Trent has told you of my problem?"

Mr Verity nodded and looked around the living room. It was one of four rooms which made up the Barkers' hotel suite, the others were their bedroom with *en suite* bathroom and Miss Cooper's room. The furniture was sparse but clean and neat: two armchairs by the warm hearth, a round table with three chairs by the window overlooking Henrietta Street, an untouched bureau in the corner, a tapestried fire screen, and potted plants. Hung upon the chimney breast, against the cream and brown-striped wallpaper, was a monochrome photograph of a handsome gentleman in his early twenties. He stood with his hand upon a table, a drawn-back curtain over his right shoulder, and a painted countryside scene behind him. The portrait was kept in a bronze-painted, wooden frame with hand-carved floral embellishment.

"I must apologise for your wasted journey and time, Mr Verity, Miss Dexter. As you can see, the portrait is as it should be and has been since we arrived in London." Mrs Barker released a deep sigh. "I fear I was in too much haste to call upon the Bow Street Society's assistance. I'll pay your fee, of course."

"If you'll permit me, Mrs Barker, I'd still like to

examine the portrait," Miss Dexter said, her voice both unobtrusive and reassuring in its gentleness.

"By all means," Mrs Barker replied with a soft smile and relaxation of her shoulders.

Miss Dexter stood and, stepping onto the hearth's tiled floor, reached up to lift the frame off its hook. Placing it upon the cushioned seat of her armchair, she held its top with one hand and leaned forward to inspect its front. "The photograph's clarity and tonal depth suggest dry gelatin plates were used. That means we may be able to get copies if needed." She turned the portrait toward the firelight and tilted it backward while she inspected its bottom corners. Seeing only the photograph, she hummed and laid the frame face first against the armchair's backrest. Next, she slipped her fingernails between the frame and the layer of thick, paper backing that kept the photograph in place. For a second time she leaned forward but, this time, inspected the corners of the photograph's rear. "Here we are," Miss Dexter beamed, "E.F. Langdon of Regent Street, London. He must've captured Mr Downton's likeness." She returned the paper backing and, with Mr Verity's assistance, rehung the portrait. "I would very much like to visit Mr Langdon. He may be able to provide us with additional information."

Mr Verity dropped down into his armchair with a soft grunt. "I agree." Once Miss Dexter sat across from him, and Mrs Barker had taken a chair at the table, he enquired, "Was your late husband a generous man? I don't want to talk out of turn, but it could be important if he left you some money of your own."

Mrs Barker frowned as the shadow of confusion fell upon her features, again. "Could it be, though…? I don't see how…" She looked to the portrait and took some courage from its continued mundaneness. "But… yes, he was very generous, Mr Verity. I have a yearly allowance from his estate. It remains my property until my own death, when it reverts to Jeffrey's only living blood relative; a niece in America."

Mr Verity slipped his crooked finger through his beard to scratch the underside of his chin. "Miss Trent told us you'd seen wet footprints coming from the portrait, too. Have they come back?"

Mrs Barker shook her head. "And no one else has ever seen them. Perhaps Creighton is right in his assertion I'm allowing my irrational feelings of guilt to overcome my rationality."

"We don't know that until we do some checking of our own," Mr Verity replied. "In my experience, spirits and phantoms come out when it's dark. I want to come back tonight, then, to watch the portrait and see what it does—if anything."

Mrs Barker looked to the window as tension crept into her body. "Impossible, I'm afraid…" She took in several shallow breaths and stood, her fingers toying with the lace of her cuff. "Creighton and I are attending a Gilbert and Sullivan opera at the Savoy Theatre tonight. Miss Cooper—my maid—will still be visiting her family." She crossed the room and reached for the door. "I really do think I've wasted your time—"

"I don't," Mr Verity retorted in an authoritative tone. Mrs Barker stopped with her hand upon the doorknob and looked back sharply. Seeing this, and the wideness of her eyes, Mr Verity leaned upon his cane and heaved himself onto his feet. Miss Dexter rose, too, and walked behind him as he shuffled toward their client. "You're afraid. That's okay, lass. We want to stop you being afraid, but we can't do that if you don't let us come back tonight."

"B-But the theatre…Creighton…" Mrs Barker mumbled.

"Give us a key now, and we'll let ourselves in," Mr Verity replied.

"We'll slip it under the door once we're finished," Miss Dexter added.

"If the portrait's haunted, as you fear it is, Jeffrey might leave it when you're not here. I'd like to see that happen for myself. He'll probably manifest himself if he doesn't think anyone's watching," Mr Verity explained.

Mrs Barker pursed her lips together and shivered. "You really think he'd…?"

"*If* he's there, yes," Mr Verity replied.

Mrs Barker released a soft sob and pressed a clenched hand to her lips. As her entire body trembled, she whispered, "Will you… will you tell him I'm sorry?" Her hand slipped from the doorknob, and she walked toward Mr Verity with tears in her eyes. "That I never meant…?"

Mr Verity closed the distance between them. "I will. I promise."

Mrs Barker gave a sad smile. "*Thank* you…" She sniffed hard and pressed the back of her hand to her lips. "Thank you." Taking out her handkerchief, she dabbed at her eyes as she walked past Mr Verity and took a key from the mantel shelf. "Here," she pressed it into Miss Dexter's hand. "Please also tell him how much I love him…?"

Miss Dexter gave a gentle nod and squeezed their client's hand. "I shall."

III

"Mr Jeffrey Downton… his likeness was captured around a year and a half ago, you said?" Mr Langdon enquired while he browsed through his store of used plates. Mr Langdon was in his mid-forties with short, chestnut-brown hair combed with a right-side parting. His build was lean, and his height exceeded six feet. Thus, his appearance was akin to a malnourished giant. The soft drawl of his voice, and warm, brown eyes gave him a genteel air, however.

"Yes, he was alone at the time," Miss Dexter replied. She stood beside Mr Langdon as he searched. She recognised the plates as the factory-produced, glass kind coated in gelatine, containing silver salts. Each one of Mr Langdon's plates depicted the ghostly visage of individuals, couples, or family groups. They were housed within wooden frames—to prevent accidental breakage or scratching—which had the name(s) of the subject(s) and the date of capture written in pencil on their top sides. Mr Langdon lifted each plate from its dedicated slot and read the label against the weak light of his kerosene lamp. Miss Dexter watched him with keen interest as she continued, "We've seen his portrait and your address on its back."

The small room in which the two met sat adjacent to the larger one that acted as his studio proper. Located on the first floor of Mr Langdon's printers' shop, the studio was accessed by a set of narrow steps in the shop's back parlour. The ceiling between this floor and the attic had been removed to allow the daylight to pour in through the windows. A thick, black velvet curtain, drawn across the doorway of the small room, blotted out this light to ensure the plates weren't faded. Pieces of scenery rested against the studio's walls behind faux stone pillars in the Grecian style, a chaise lounge, various shaped and sized chairs, and numerous potted ferns and bushes. Mr Verity sat on the chaise with both hands upon the silver skull-shaped handle of his walking cane between his knees. He looked over the stacked scenery and one in particular caught his eye.

"I've found it," Mr Langdon said and held the framed plate over the weak lamp for Miss Dexter to examine. "Mr Jeffrey Downton, his likeness was captured on the fifth of May 1895."

"Thank you, Mr Langdon," Miss Dexter replied. "We may need a copy of it later."

"Certainly," Mr Langdon said with a smile and placed the plate into its slot. Shutting the lid of the trunk used to store the plates, he held the curtain open for the young artist to walk under. Following her into the studio—allowing the curtain to drop behind him as he did so—he enquired from Mr Verity, "Can I be of any further assistance?"

"We wish to know the name of anyone who has recently requested for a countryside scene, table, and curtain to be photographed," Miss Dexter replied.

"*That* one," Mr Verity added and pointed to the scenery he'd noticed, a country lane framed by trees. It was half-hidden behind another of a Grecian garden. "That's the same one Mr Downton had, wasn't it?"

Mr Langdon wandered over and lifted the garden scene to scrutinise the countryside one. "I believe so, yes." He rested one arm across his stomach and then his other elbow upon his arm while he tapped his chin with three fingers. "I think I recall… Yes, around six weeks ago, a young woman had a photograph of this scenery, the table, and the curtain taken. I can't believe it never occurred to me that it would be the same in Mr Downton's photograph."

"But why would it?" Mr Verity pointed out.

Mr Langdon gave a slight shrug of his shoulder.

"Can you recall her name?" Miss Dexter enquired.

Mr Langdon hummed and pulled some pince-nez from his trouser pocket. Crossing to his desk, he balanced the pince-nez upon his nose and flipped through a ledger until he found the relevant entry. Rather than read aloud the name, though, he peered over his pince-nez at the two. "Forgive me, Mr Verity, Miss Dexter, but *why* do you want this information?"

"We believe she might be using the portrait to frighten someone," Mr Verity replied.

"Most cruelly," Miss Dexter added.

"I see…" Mr Langdon frowned. "How terrible… Well, I think this is who you're looking for." He spun the ledger around so they could see the entry for themselves. "Miss Doris Cooper."

IV

The hotel was quieter in the evening; the majority of its guests had departed for the restaurants and theatres. Thus, Mr Verity and Miss Dexter didn't encounter anyone but the hotel employees when they traversed the stairs and corridors to room thirteen. Yet, as they turned the corner, a gentleman in evening wear left the Barkers' suite. He was in his late forties with thin, pale-blond hair, dark-blue eyes, and a stocky build. Mr Verity retreated and ushered Miss Dexter to join him. When they next heard the heavy tread of the gentleman's approach, Mr Verity leaned forward and feigned a coughing fit.

While Miss Dexter rubbed his back, the gentleman hurried around the corner but stopped when he came upon the sudden obstruction. Taking a brief moment to compose himself, he then walked around them and down the corridor to the stairwell door. Despite their brief encounter, Mr Verity doubted the gentleman had paid them much heed. His eyes had shifted in all directions, with sweat on his forehead, and his evening suit dishevelled. When he heard the stairwell door close, Mr Verity shuffled across the corridor and said, "The window." Miss Dexter followed, and they peered down at Henrietta Street. A hansom cab waited by the curb and, within minutes, the gentleman emerged from the hotel and climbed inside. Though they couldn't hear what he said to the driver—if anything—the cab pulled away in the direction of the Savoy Theatre. A heartbeat later, the Bow Street Society's own cab passed beneath the window to follow the first.

"Mr Barker, I presume?" Miss Dexter whispered.

"Probably," Mr Verity replied.

"He looked frightened."

"He did." Mr Verity shuffled back to room thirteen. "I wonder if Mr Downton showed himself earlier than expected." When he opened the door, though, the shaft of light from the hallway came to rest upon a lifeless form lying upon the hearth rug.

Miss Dexter gasped, rushed inside, and knelt beside it. Finding an unconscious woman in her early twenties, Miss Dexter tried to rouse her with a shake of her shoulder. When she pulled away her hand, she found blood smeared across her palm. "Mr Verity!"

The spiritualist shuffled over and, seeing the blood, got down on one knee. As he gripped his cane to steady himself with one hand, his other reached around to hover by the woman's lips. "She still breathes," he remarked. "Where's the blood coming from?"

"Here, I think," Miss Dexter replied, indicating where an ornate hat pin protruded from the woman's shoulder.

"Don't move her," Mr Verity instructed and heaved himself back onto his feet. The lamp upon the table was lit with a small flame. He therefore increased its size to illuminate the room proper while Miss Dexter closed the door. As she returned to the fallen woman, though, she noticed a photograph tucked beneath her arm. Its frame was identical to the one around Mr Downton's portrait, but its content comprised of just the painted countryside scenery, a table, and a curtain.

"This must be the photograph taken by Mr Langdon several weeks ago," Miss Dexter observed and slipped it out from under the fallen woman.

"And this Miss Doris Cooper, then?" Mr Verity enquired as he glanced to the woman.

"But where's Mr Downton's portrait?" Miss Dexter had looked to the chimney breast to find it bare. "Mr Barker wasn't carrying anything when he left, and Mrs Barker knew we were returning this evening."

A sudden groan from the woman distracted them, however.

Miss Dexter moved backward and stood behind the armchair, the photograph grasped against her chest. She and Mr Verity watched the woman lift her head, open her eyes, and push herself up onto her knees. A second groan escaped her while she sat upon her heels but, when she reached to hold her head, her body jerked as she yelped. She then clutched her wounded shoulder and noticed the two Bow Streeters. Her other arm immediately wrapped around her stomach, and she shuffled around on her behind to put her back to the cold hearth.

"Who are you?" the woman demanded.

"Miss Georgina Dexter and Mr Virgil Verity of the Bow Street Society, Miss Cooper," Miss Dexter replied.

"How did you know it was me?" Miss Cooper enquired, stunned.

"Mere assumption, I'm afraid," Miss Dexter replied. "Why did Mr Barker harm you?"

Miss Cooper dropped her head and pursed her lips. In due course she replied, without taking her eyes off the other armchair, "I've no idea." Yet, almost at once, she straightened, parted her lips, and scrutinised the floor to her left and right in quick succession.

"I have it here," Miss Dexter said and turned the frame around to show Miss Cooper. "Why was it under your arm? Were you about to hang it in place of Mr Downton's portrait?" Miss Dexter stepped around the armchair and rested the frame's edge upon its arm. "That's how you've led Mrs Barker to believe Mr Downton has been leaving his photograph, isn't it? By switching his for this one and— in collusion with Mr Barker—insist Mr Downton's portrait was still intact and visible to you both."

"Don't forget the wet footprints," Mr Verity interjected.

"Which would explain why Mr Barker harmed you," Miss Dexter resumed. "*Why*, Miss Cooper? *Why* would you be so cruel to your mistress?"

Miss Cooper bowed her head but kept her arm wrapped tight around her stomach.

"Oh…" Miss Dexter said as the realisation dawned upon her. "You are with child."

"Mr Barker's?" Mr Verity enquired and shuffled forward to sit on a chair by the table. At Miss Cooper's curt nod, he continued, "It was dark in here when we found you. If it was the same when Mr Barker put that hat pin in your shoulder, he probably thought he'd got your neck."

"We saw him in the hallway," Miss Dexter said. "He looked so frightened we thought Mr Downton's ghost may have appeared before him. It would appear, instead, like he thought he'd murdered you."

"All of what we've found out so far has you behind the portrait's happenings," Mr Verity began. "You had the new photograph taken at Mr Langdon's studio, and we found you with it under your arm. When Mr Barker finds out you live, he'll make sure the police get rid of you for him."

"And, unfortunately, a gentleman's word is worth more than a servant's," Miss Dexter pointed out, concerned.

"You must help me," Miss Cooper pleaded as she leaned toward them. "It's true, all of it, but I can't let my baby be born in Newgate. *Please*, I only agreed to help him because he promised we'd be together once his wife was put in an asylum. I was trying to save us from the workhouse."

Mr Verity took in a slow, deep breath. "Our priority is Mrs Barker and her happiness. Exposing Mr Barker's cruel scheme would help us with that, but you must confess your part, too."

"Will the Bow Street Society protect me and my child?"

"We can't guarantee that, Miss Cooper," Miss Dexter replied, "but we'll endeavour to do our best for you both."

"Okay." Miss Cooper grimaced. "Tell me what to do."

"You can begin by showing us where Mr Downton's portrait is," Miss Dexter replied.

V

The sound of wheels and hooves over cobblestones came through the open living room window of the Barkers' suite as a cab approached. When both ceased, the metallic scrape of a bolt filled the otherwise silent street, followed by the bounce of two doors against their hinges. Next, a male's deep voice was heard to instruct, "Go inside where it's warm, Clementine. I'll be along presently."

Mrs Barker replied, "But I... yes, darling." Her heeled shoes tapped against the damp stone as she climbed the steps and entered the hotel.

Meanwhile, Mr Barker enquired, "How much did we agree upon, again?" A reply was given but the words were indistinguishable at that distance. The next to be understood were therefore Mr Barker's, "Are you *quite* certain of that?"

"She'll be here anytime now," Mr Verity whispered from the right of the suite's door. Miss Dexter—who sat by the window—swallowed and rubbed her clasped hands together in her lap as she nodded. She next watched Miss Cooper open the suite's door ajar and peer out into the deserted hallway beyond. All three held their breaths as they listened for the rustle of Mrs Barker's skirts and the distinct tap of her heels.

"I don't care what you *think*, we agreed on a much lower price than *that*," Mr Barker said. "You can't cheat me simply because I'm a visitor to London."

"With all due respect, sir, the price I've said is the price we agreed," a second raised—but calm—voice replied. Miss Dexter recognised it as belonging to the Bow Street Society's cabman, Mr Samuel Snyder.

"You people don't know the meaning of respect,"

Mr Barker retorted.

Miss Cooper widened the gap in the door as she heard the stairwell's one close, followed by Mrs Barker's heels against the carpet, and the swift rustle of her skirts. "Mrs Barker!" she whispered when she saw her mistress come into view. "Mrs Barker, *hurry*."

"*Doris*?" Mrs Barker gasped but rushed to greet her nonetheless. "What's happened?"

Miss Cooper took her mistress by the arm and led her inside. "There's no time to explain, but the Bow Street Society is here, and they need your help."

Mrs Barker glanced to Miss Dexter by the window, and then Mr Verity when he shuffled up beside her. "You do?" Mrs Barker enquired from him. "Why? Did Jeffrey not show himself?"

"No, and I don't think he ever will," Mr Verity admitted with a deep frown. "But there *is* a dark influence on your life, and it can be exorcised if you'll do as we ask."

"That's the fare, sir. I can fetch a constable, if you want," Mr Snyder said.

"Y-Yes, of course, Mr Verity. What do you want me to do?" Mrs Barker enquired.

"No…" Mr Barker sighed. "There'll be no need for that."

"Miss Cooper is going to lie on the rug by the hearth," Mr Verity began. "When she's ready, we want you to scream as loud as you can and then lie on the floor like you've fainted."

Mrs Barker stared at him a moment. "W-Will you repeat that, please?"

"*Please*, ma'am, there's no time to explain," Miss Cooper urged as she led Mrs Barker toward the hearth and lay down. "You must trust them or all is lost." Turning onto her stomach, she positioned herself to mimic the manner in which she'd been found earlier. As she did so, though, the hat pin—that was still embedded into her shoulder—was revealed. Mrs Barker gasped in horror and reached down to retrieve it. Yet, Miss Dexter lunged forward and gripped her wrist to stay her.

"But it-it's the one from my hat," Mrs Barker explained as they heard shoes scrape against stone outside. When Mrs Barker felt around in her hat, though, she widened her eyes and pulled out the very hat pin she thought she'd lost. "I-I don't understand…" She looked to Miss Dexter. "…What is *happening* here?"

"Your husband attacked Miss Cooper this evening," Miss Dexter whispered. "I promise we shall explain at length but first, you *must* do as we ask."

Mrs Barker trembled as she leaned against Miss Dexter.

"*Quickly*, now," Mr Verity urged from his spot by the suite's door.

Mrs Barker looked around, as if in a daze, but, finally, gave a slow nod. "Very well… I shall do as you ask."

Miss Dexter smiled and gave Mrs Barker's hand a gentle squeeze. While she moved to stand with her back against the wall to the left of the suite's door, Mrs Barker put herself at Miss Cooper's feet, filled her lungs, and released a blood-curdling scream. Immediately afterward, she sat upon the floor and lay back, her arms limp above her head, in a feigned faint.

"That came from my suite!" Mr Barker cried from the stairwell.

Those in the suite listened to the chaos that

followed—the frenzied footfalls of Mr Barker running up the stairs with several others, and the holla—from somewhere inside the hotel—for a constable to be fetched.

"Room thirteen!" Mr Barker boomed as he and the others erupted from the stairwell and into the corridor. "*Hurry*!"

Many feet thundered along the carpet, and Mr Barker was the first to appear when the suite's door burst open. Rather than rush inside, though, he stopped dead in the doorway, thereby preventing the others from both seeing and accessing the scene of devastation beyond. "Oh dear God!" He cried. "Clementine, what have you *done*?!"

"Let us in, sir—" an unfamiliar male voice—possibly the hotel's desk clerk—requested from the corridor.

Mr Barker then stepped forward, as the weight of bodies unbalanced him, but quickly turned and gripped the doorframe. "*No*! Please… she's my wife, and she's not well. Let me talk to her. I don't want her harming herself, too."

Those in the corridor talked amongst themselves for a moment. A sudden yell from the stairwell then informed them a constable would arrive soon, however.

"In that case… please proceed, sir," the unfamiliar male voice told Mr Barker.

"*Thank* you, gentlemen," Mr Barker replied. He stepped back to close the door but once it was locked, he turned upon his heel and strode over to the right-hand armchair. The cushion upon its seat was lifted and a large, square object wrapped in black cloth was revealed beneath. Mr Barker pulled it out from its hiding place and, whilst he held it in one hand, slipped the framed photograph out from beneath Miss Cooper's arm with his other. The latter was then laid upon the armchair's base and covered with the cushion before he uncovered the former. As the cloth fell away, Miss Dexter and Mr Verity saw Mr Jeffrey Downton's distinct portrait in the dim lamplight. They watched as Mr Barker tucked it under Miss Cooper's arm, stepped across to his wife, and ran his fingertips over her hat in search of her pin. "Where *is* it?" he hissed.

"Lost something, darling?" Mrs Barker suddenly enquired as she opened her eyes, sat up, and held the lost pin aloft for him to see.

Mr Barker stumbled back in fright and fell upon the armchair, his eyes wide and the colour draining from his face. "C-Clementine! Y-You're—?!"

"*Enlightened*, Creighton," Mrs Barker replied with disgust.

Mr Barker looked, then, to Miss Cooper as she, too, sat up and glared at him. He visibly trembled at the sight but, though he moved his lips, no sound came out. Meanwhile, Mr Verity unlocked and opened the suite's door to permit the others to enter. At the same time, Miss Dexter turned up the lamp and waved down to Mr Snyder to let him know they were unhurt. Mr Barker's wide eyes darted from her, to Mr Verity, to his wife, to Miss Cooper, to those gathered in the doorway, and back again to his wife. "Y-You tricked me!" His jaw muscles tensed. "What the *devil's* going on?!"

"Fraud, Mr Barker, and a cruel one at that," Mr Verity replied with a grave expression and sombre tone. "A fraud concocted by *you* and your *lover*, Miss Doris Cooper."

Mr Barker glanced to the doorway as the constable hurried inside and stopped behind the others.

"I was called for," the constable explained.

"You were. Arrest these people," Mr Barker demanded.

"Constable, I'm Mr Virgil Verity of the Bow Street Society, and this is my friend, fellow member, and freelance artist Miss Georgina Dexter. Mrs Barker hired our group to discover if the portrait of her late husband was haunted or not. We've discovered it wasn't, and that her husband and her maid had been switching the portrait—with one showing only scenery, a table, and curtain—to make her think her late husband had been leaving his own photograph. They also made wet footprints on the carpet to convince her even more."

"You what?" the constable enquired, confused.

"And why would I want to do something as idiotic as *that*?" Mr Barker challenged.

"To control your wife's allowance from her late husband's estate," Miss Dexter replied and moved to be at Mr Verity's side. "She told us she inherited the money as her own and, when she dies, it reverts to her late husband's niece who lives in America. If Mrs Barker was committed to an asylum, though, you could keep the allowance for yourself."

"But if that was his intention, why did he attack Doris?" Mrs Barker enquired, confused.

"She knew of what he was doing, and she carries his bairn, so those are two reasons," Mr Verity explained. "The third is, he could tell the police you were driven mad by the idea of your late husband haunting you, and you killed Miss Cooper because of that madness. That's why he used a hat pin the same as the one you wore tonight—to make sure the police thought you'd used it to kill Miss Cooper—and why he tried to steal yours from you when he thought you'd fainted. He switched the photograph without Mr Downton in it for the one with him and hid the first, so you wouldn't be believed when you told the police you didn't see Mr Downton in the photograph when you found it on Miss Cooper's body."

"Don't be *absurd*," Mr Barker retorted. "I was at the Savoy Theatre *all* evening, watching a Gilbert & Sullivan opera. Ask our friends, Mr and Mrs Weatherall, ask the ushers at the theatre. I never left once."

"But you did," Mr Verity replied. "Miss Dexter and me saw you leave this room when you were meant to be out."

"And the Bow Street Society's own cab, driven by our friend Mr Samuel Snyder, followed yours when it left," Miss Dexter interjected. "He's outside, now, Constable, if you'd like to ask him where Mr Barker went after he left here." She shifted her gaze to Mr Barker. "From the corridor, Mr Verity and I watched you get into the cab Mr Snyder's followed."

Mr Barker grimaced.

"I'll do that, don't you worry, Miss," the constable replied. "Where's the photograph without Mr Downton in it?"

"Underneath the cushion Mr Barker is sitting on," Miss Dexter replied.

The constable straightened his tunic and stepped around the group to approach Mr Barker. "Stand up, please, sir."

Mr Barker glanced from the constable, to his wife, to Miss Cooper, and back again. With a deep sigh, he put his hands upon the chair's arms and stood. The constable at once took a firm grip of him and tossed the cushion onto the floor. Mr Jeffrey Downton's eyes stared up at them. "I think you'd better come along with me, sir." The constable picked up the photograph, pulled Mr Barker away from the armchair, and led him to the suite's open door. "I'll need you all to come along, too. Statements will have to be taken at the police station."

"We'll bring Mrs Barker and Miss Cooper with us in Mr Snyder's cab," Mr Verity replied. The constable agreed and frog-marched Mr Barker downstairs. Mr Verity and Miss Dexter meanwhile helped up Mrs Barker and Miss Cooper from the floor. They would then accompany them on a tense cab ride, followed by incredible discussions with a most perplexed Metropolitan Police Inspector.

Enjoyed the book? Please show your support by writing a review.

DISCOVER MORE AT...
www.bowstreetsociety.com

Notes from the author

Spoiler alert

This is the second volume of the *Bow Street Society Casebook*. *The Case of The Shrinking Shopkeeper & Other Stories* being the first. I'm amazed ideas for them keep coming to mind. The starting point of the thought process is usually one or two specific Bow Street Society members and their professions. Regardless of whether I'm writing a short story or a book, the test for any Bow Street Society mystery plot is: can the members I've chosen draw upon their professions' skills or knowledge to solve the case? If not, the idea is reworked or discarded. If, on the other hand, an idea lends itself to being the focus of an investigation by a particular member and their profession, I then determine if—historically speaking—such an investigation could've been plausible. These two steps were completed with each of the stories in this collection.

Prior to writing *The Case of The Desperate Deed*, I'd adhered to the rule of having four parts to each short story. *Desperate Deed* breaks this rule, but it wasn't intended for a casebook collection when it was first conceived. At the time, I was a member of a Facebook writers' group who were working toward publishing an anthology of mixed genre stories under the heading 'New Beginnings.' The first few drafts of *Desperate Deed* were comprised of four parts. When the anthology's editors had read it though, they wanted more period detail to help them fall in love with the era. This is why part one of *Desperate Deed* follows Mrs Emillia Kinsley's journey from Charing Cross station to Bow Street, rather than the consultation with Miss Trent in part two.

Unfortunately, the anthology was never completed. The addition of a fifth part in *Desperate Deed* enabled me to permit myself to extend future stories in the same way, however. This, in turn, gave me the capacity to write mysteries which were more complex than *The Case of The Shrinking Shopkeeper*, but simpler than *The Case of The Curious Client*.

I also broke another of my own steadfast casebook rules in *The Case of The Desperate Deed*—never introduce a brand-new Bow Street Society member to the reader. As the anthology's theme was 'New Beginnings,' it made sense for my story's new beginning to come in the form of the Bow Street Society gaining a new member. Though he doesn't undergo the official process of joining the Society (and there is one, it's just not been revealed in the books, yet) he does get invited to do so.

My intention is to include Mr Lorne Cheshire in a future book, but I expect the other members shan't be pleased when they discover the origins of his membership. In *The Case of The Curious Client*, Miss Trent hints at a theft Mr Percy Locke may, or may not, have been involved with. Mr Locke's housebreaking abilities are also unusual for a stage magician. That being said, Mr Locke's expertise are often utilised—his breaking into the Queshire Department store in *The Case of The Lonesome Lushington*, for example—so Mr Cheshire's past may not be held against him for long. His knowledge of jewellery manufacture and precious stones could also be useful in a theft-based mystery.

The title and focus of *The Case of The Scandalous Somnambulist* was inspired by the Victorians' obsession with sleepwalkers, specifically beautiful women whose affliction put them in peril. A chapter in the nonfiction book, *Strange Victoriana*, describes many so-called "true" instances of sleepwalking women almost plunging to their deaths. These instances were reported in the *Illustrated Police News* at the time. Incidentally, the *Illustrated Police News* had no association with the police. Instead, it reported macabre or fantastical crimes and events in a sensational way. Rather than write a simple case of a woman almost sleepwalking to her death, though, I wanted an element of intrigue. This came in the form of Mr Truman overhearing his wife in another man's bedroom, but not knowing of his new wife's affliction.

When it came to *The Case of The Peculiar Portrait*, several variations of the mystery's central focus were considered. My first idea was similar to the end one in that it was a painting purported to "lose" some of its elements. Rather than being taken off the wall and switched, though, the painting's canvas was rotated within its frame by someone on the other side of the partition wall the painting was hung upon. The believability of this idea was low, however, due to the fact the Bow Street Society members would examine the wall during their investigation. My second idea was to keep the painting but have it on a looped canvas that slid under the propulsion of a music box's brass cylinders. The box's music would have masked the sound of the paper moving. Again, the impracticality of this idea led me to abandon it. The idea I went with is simple but believable, and gave Mr Verity his first outing beyond the books.

Miss Georgina Dexter's appearance in *The Case of The Peculiar Portrait* was another breakage of my casebook steadfast rules: only featuring members once in a Casebook collection. The first draft of the *Peculiar Portrait* had Mr Verity accompanied by Lady Katheryne

Owston. As Mrs Barker's problem centred on a photograph, it was more likely Miss Trent would've assigned Miss Dexter—who has experience of photographic development—than Lady Owston. All Lady Owston could've brought to the investigation was her social class and gender. Furthermore, if Lady Owston had joined Mr Verity, I would've felt compelled to have Miss Agnes Webster, Lady Owston's secretary, accompany her. Again, there was little reason for Miss Webster to be involved in the case, either. To put it plainly, their skills and knowledge would've gone to waste. I therefore think the Verity and Dexter combination was the better option, despite Miss Dexter having already accompanied Dr Locke in *The Case of The Scandalous Somnambulist* (albeit in a lesser role).

~ T.G. Campbell
November 2018

MORE BOW STREET SOCIETY

The Case of The Shrinking Shopkeeper
& Other Stories
(Bow Street Society Casebook Volume 1)

An illusionist, medical doctor, veterinary surgeon, architect, freelance journalist, solicitor, artist, cabman, secretary, and newspaper journalist are all called upon by the Society's clerk, Miss Rebecca Trent, to investigate a plethora of peculiar puzzles. From a sweet-shop owner who believes he's losing height at an alarming rate to the mysterious disappearance of a woman from inside a carriage. From a beloved family pet being the subject of a bizarre accusation, to a conversation with a dead man, to an unjust dismissal from a toy maker's. Each Bow Street

Society member must draw upon their knowledge and expertise to solve these baffling problems once and for all…

In this collection:

**The Case of the Shrinking Shopkeeper
The Case of the Winchester Wife
The Case of the Perilous Pet
The Case of the Eerie Encounter
The Case of the Christmas Crisis**

*On sale now in eBook and paperback from Amazon.
Also available for free download via Kindle Unlimited.*

**The Case of The Russian Rose
& Other Stories
*(Bow Street Society Casebook Volume 3)***

The Case of the Russian Rose & Other Stories is the third
volume of shorter mysteries to feature the group. Wherein
they must solve peculiar problems posed by their colourful
array of clients, such as: "how is a pocket picked in an
empty train compartment?" and "How did a bullet vanish
from a gun without being fired?" These are just some of
the questions the Bow Street Society must answer to
expose the fantastic truths behind these bizarre cases

In this collection:

The Case of the Pesky Passenger
The Case of the Taken Teacup
The Case of the Russian Rose
The Case of the Crooked Cottage
The Case of the Baffled Bride

On sale now in eBook and paperback from Amazon.
Also available for free download via Kindle Unlimited.

**The Case of The Gentleman's Gambit
& Other Stories
*(Bow Street Society Casebook Volume 4)***

The Case of the Gentleman's Gambit & Other Stories is
the fourth volume of shorter mysteries to feature the
group. Wherein they must solve peculiar problems posed
by their colourful array of clients, such as: "how did gold
vanish from a moving train without four guards seeing the
thief?", "Is a ghost from Whitechapel haunting a wealthy
woman?" and "Can playing cards be used to poison
someone?" These are just some of the questions the Bow
Street Society must answer to expose the fantastic truths
behind these bizarre cases.

In this collection:

The Case of the Terrific Theft
The Case of the Whitechapel Wraith
The Case of the Fowler Fortune
The Case of the Gentleman's Gambit
The Case of the Puma Problem

On sale now in eBook and paperback from Amazon.
Also available for free download via Kindle Unlimited.

SOURCES OF REFERENCE

A great deal of time was spent researching the historical setting of these short stories. Thus, a great deal of information about the period has been gathered, to inform me of the historical boundaries of my characters' professions and lives, which hasn't been directly referenced in this book. Where a fact, or source, has been used to inform the basis of descriptions/statements made by characters in the book, I've strived to cite said source here. Each citation includes the source's origin, the source's author, and which part of this collection the source is connected to. All rights connected to the following sources remain with their respective authors and publishers.

The Case of the Desperate Deed

Encyclopædia Britannica article, *Paste Jewelry:*
https://www.britannica.com/art/paste-jewelry
Paste gems and jewellery in the British Victorian Era

Victoria & Albert Museum's website article, *History of Fashion 1840-1900*:
http://www.vam.ac.uk/content/articles/h/history-of-fashion-1840-1900/
Mrs Kinsley's fashionable sleeves and Mr Cheshire's clean-shaven face.

Booth, Charles Booth's Maps of London Poverty East and West 1889 (reproduced by Old House Books)
Used as historical reference source for the social class of the residents of Mount Street

Lee Jackson's The Victorian Dictionary
http://www.victorianlondon.org/index-2012.htm
The following sources are all taken from The Victorian Dictionary website

"OMNIBUSES"—Reynolds' Shilling Map of London, 1895
Omnibus running times, fares, colours, and routes.

Photograph of a hansom Cab, 1896.
Description of a hansom Cab

Wey, Francis A Frenchman Sees the English in the Fifties, 1935
The size of an omnibus, passengers preferring the upper deck.

Punch, September 28, 1861
Omnibus conductors referred to as 'cads'

Greenwood, James. The Seven Curses of London, 1869
Dishonesty of Omnibus conductors and working hours.

Cassell and Company Limited, The Queen's London. A Pictorial and Descriptive Record of the Streets, Buildings, Parks and Scenery of the Great Metropolis in the Fifty-Ninth year of the reign of Her Majesty Queen Victoria, 1896
Description of the interior of Charing Cross station and Charing Cross Hotel.

The Case of the Chilling Chamber

Booth's Poverty Map:
https://booth.lse.ac.uk/map/17/-0.0994/51.5082/100/0?marker=532505,180660
Fictional location of The Rose and Thistle public house, social class of the streets surrounding The Rose and Thistle, Directions from Bow Street to Waterloo Pier via Wellington Street, Directions from Blackfriars' Pier to the fictional location of The Rose and Thistle,

Tudor Style Encyclopaedia Britannica article:
https://www.britannica.com/art/Tudor-style
Defining characteristics of Tudor architecture as defined by Mr Heath.

***

Lee Jackson's The Victorian Dictionary
http://www.victorianlondon.org/index-2012.htm
The following sources are all taken from The Victorian Dictionary website

Reynolds' Shilling Coloured Map of London, 1895, specifically the section entitled STEAMERS. London Bridge (City and Surrey sides) to Chelsea from
The steamer's route.

Dickens's Dictionary of London, by Charles Dickens, Jr., 1879 - "CAB-CHA" from
Location of the cabman shelter

The Case of the Ghastly Gallop

Cow cross Street and Turnmill Street Pages 182-202
<u>Survey of London: Volume 46, South and East Clerkenwell</u>. Originally published by London County Council, London, 2008. https://www.british-history.ac.uk/survey-london/vol46/pp182-202
Metropolitan Cattle Market and Sharp's Alley as a horse-slaughtering area

Advert for the Guardian Horse Vehicle & General Insurance Company Ltd from the British Library website.
http://www.bl.uk/onlinegallery/onlineex/evancoll/a/zoomify73788.html
Horse insurance.

***

Lee Jackson's The Victorian Dictionary
http://www.victorianlondon.org/index-2012.htm
The following sources are all taken from The Victorian
Dictionary website

**London and Londoners in the Eighteen-Fifties and
Sixties, by Alfred Rosling Bennett, 1924 - Chapter 10 -
Buildings, Beer and Bears' Grease**
Name and description of Porter.

**George Birch, The Descriptive Album of London,
c.1896**
http://www.victorianlondon.org/markets/copenhagenfields.
htm
*The trade, location, description, and name of the cattle
market.*

**The Morning Chronicle: Labour and the Poor, 1849-
50; Henry Mayhew - Letter XIII**
http://www.victorianlondon.org/mayhew/mayhew13.htm
Cow Cross yard as the largest in London

**THE MYSTERIES OF LONDON Foreword by Lee
Jackson Brief Introduction by Dick Collins CHAPTER
LXI. THE "BOOZING KEN" ONCE MORE.**
*http://www.victorianlondon.org/mysteries/mysteries-
61.htm*
Horse meat into sausages

**Cassells Household Guide, New and Revised Edition (4
Vol.) c.1880s [no date] - The Horse (1) - Introduction -
Of the Different Breeds of Horses - Of Eastern Breeds -
Western Breeds - European Horses, specifically the
section entitled "STRUCTURE OF THE HORSE" in
"THE HORSE II"**
http://www.victorianlondon.org/cassells/cassells-49.htm

Dr Alexander's findings upon examining the dead horse and Cunning Tom.

The Case of the Peculiar Portrait

Lee Jackson's The Victorian Dictionary
http://www.victorianlondon.org/index-2012.htm
The following source was taken from The Victorian Dictionary website

SAVOY THEATRE entry in Charles Dickens Jr. et al, Dickens Dictionary of London, c.1908 edition (no date; based on internal evidence)
Theatre adjoining the Savoy Hotel.

***

Encyclopaedia Britannica article, "Development of the dry plate"
http://www.britannica.com/technology/photography/Development-of-the-dry-plate
Gelatin plates and their manufacture.

SAVOY THEATRE HISTORY AND TIMELINE 1882 — 1901 The Savoy Operas
https://savoy.londontheatres.co.uk/history/
Gilbert & Sullivan operas at the Savoy Theatre.

Booth, Charles Booth's Maps of London Poverty East and West 1889 (reproduced by Old House Books)
Classification of Henrietta Street as middle class and Henrietta Street's close proximity to Bow Street.

Printed in Great Britain
by Amazon